JUNGLE SERIES

Written By LI DI

Mongoose!

A story about
struggle and wisdom

Mongoose!

Mongoose!

...nus Press USA

Original Title: 《獴！獴！獴！》

Original book by The Writers Publishing House Co.,Ltd.

MONGOOSE! MONGOOSE! MONGOOSE!

Written by Li Di

Translated by Haiwang Yuan

Designed by Brandy Ding

First edition 2022

ISBN: 978-1-61612-145-7

Contents

Chapter 1

Nimbly pushing aside branches of small trees blocking his way, a ruddy-faced man in black shirt and pants strode along a narrow, winding mountain path, with dead twigs and fallen leaves crunching beneath his feet.

Barehanded and unencumbered, he had only a cloth sack around his waist.

A startled biting midge fluttered out of a shrub and threw itself by chance into the ruddy-faced man's open mouth as he was breathing heavily.

The ruddy-faced man tried to spit it out but in vain. So, he was going to take it out.

He had just placed his fingers into his mouth when suddenly a hand reached out from a shrub and held his chin up.

The hand was thrusted out as swiftly as a knife leaving its scabbard.

Immediately following the hand, a word sharper than the edge of a knife was jammed into ruddy-faced man's ears.

"Don't move!"

The ruddy-faced man stood motionless.

And he could not budge anyway.

It was because his fingers were gripped tightly between his teeth when his chin was pushed up abruptly.

The hand holding his chin up was very strong.

The ruddy-faced man suffered an excruciating pain caused by his own bite on his fingers.

He looked askance and saw a bulky man with a pair of eagle eyes.

"What're you looking at?" The eagle-eyed man yelled. "Hand anything valuable to me like you do to your father!"

While yelling, the eagle-eyed man reached out to grab the ruddy-faced man's cloth sack.

He grappled something empty.

There was nothing in the cloth sack.

He dug his hand into the ruddy-faced man's shirt to fumble.

As if there were something burning in it...

He instantly retracted his hand involuntarily.

What his hand had touched was not fire, but a handgun!

An icy-old handgun!

The eagle-eyed man lost no time in thrusting his hand into his own shirt.

Before he had time to do so, an iron palm swooped down and whammed him right on the forehead.

The blow immediately caused his nose to bleed and his eyes to see stars.

The eagle-eyed man toddled back while his hand let go the ruddy-faced man's chin.

While he was struggling to keep his footing, an iron foot flew over landed on his chest with a thump.

What a flying kick! It must have 1,000 kg.m/s of momentum!

The unexpected discovery of a gun had already made him suffer a near mental breakdown, and the strikes of a palm and a kick knocked him completely off balance.

He fell on his back like a wooden door panel.

The ruddy-faced man lunged forward and stepped on the eagle-eyed man's chest. With his toes, the former hooked a dagger from the latter's shirt, kicked it up into the air, and received it with his hand.

Wow, what a thin and sharp blade!

Anyone to be killed by such an overly thin and sharp blade won't feel the slightest pain.

From the reflection on the blade, the ruddy-faced man saw his cheeks smeared with dirt and grass bits.

"My hero, I beg you to show mercy!" screamed the eagle-eyed man under his feet. "I became a robber because I'm in the hole. Tell me your name, and I'll repay you for your kindness in the future."

The ruddy-faced man looked frighteningly stern.

The sharp dagger cast a streak of faint light on his stern face.

"I didn't have to kill you, but you're knowing what you're not supposed to. Since you've taught me a swift and accurate move with the dagger, I'll let you know who I am before your death. My name's Gebu!"

As soon as he finished, he shoved the thin blade into the eagle-eyed man's chest.

It went right into his heart.

Such a move with such a speed left the victim no chance to whimper.

The eagle-eyed man died in silence.

He should not have known that Gebu had a gun in his shirt.

Gebu looked up. He saw only one hill lying ahead between him and his destination.

Chapter 2

He stood on the slope of the hill, his black shirt flutte-ring in the wind.

It was fluttering like the wings of a hawk…

Gebu was like a hawk.

But people from the stockage village preferred calling him Mongoose.

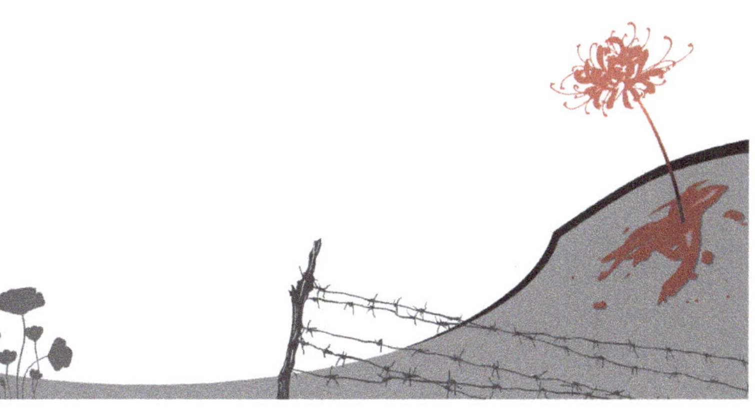

And because of his ruddy face, they nicknamed him Red-faced Mongoose.

In zoology, the red-faced mongoose refers to a small mammal living in the depth of mountain forests. Resembling the weasel, it has a sleek body, short legs, a tapered snout, and small ears. Its fur is of the brown color with a tint of green. Its eyes especially bright, red-faced mongoose is known to kill venomous snakes with a fierce and yet dexterous stratagem. It is, therefore, regarded as a natural enemy of vipers.

When attacking a viper, a red-faced mongoose will bristle up its long hair to make itself look twice bigger. It does so to menace its opponent before a ferocious battle ensues…

With its bright eyes glaring, the mongoose circles around the venomous snake. It is circling and circling when it suddenly pounces upon its prey like a blast. After quickly gripping the esophagus part of the snake in its teeth, it leaps away as fast as lightning. It immediately springs back and took another bite before leaping away again. It attacks and dodges, dodges and attacks in an ultimate test of prowess until the reptile, no matter how ferocious it is, gets so exhausted that it can no longer raise its head and ends up having its lower body separated by the mongoose's sharp teeth.

Mongooses are not immune to the snake venom.

Once bitten by a venomous snake, a mongoose will die after the venom gets into its circulatory and nervous systems.

With a body as agile as that of a swimming fish, a mongoose can hardly be bitten anyway.

In case it is bitten, it only loses some of the bristling hair to the snake's fangs.

Whirlwind biting attacks and lightning backward leaps constitute a mongoose's unique tactic of offense.

In terms of the body structure, a mongoose, with a powerful circulatory system unique to mammals, is highly adaptable to strenuous movements and therefore superior to cold-blooded reptiles. In a tug-of-war, a mongoose can always maintain its stamina and finally gets the upper hand of its serpent opponent.

Mongooses fall into several species in the forests here. Among them, the red-faced species is the sworn enemy of venomous snakes.

Soon after its birth, it attacks a snake as it sees it.

The villagers gave Gebu the nickname Red-faced Mongoose because he was also a sworn enemy of venomous snakes.

An expert snake catcher, he knew all kinds of snakes, hunted them as his job, and feared no snake bites.

In the past decade or so, he had caught countless snakes, a feat that earned him the Red-faced Mongoose nickname.

Treating snakes as weak and defenseless, ethnic Aini[1] hunters customarily do not chase and kill them, which they deem to be an act of cowardice.

In fact, venomous snakes are hard to deal with, and not every hunter is up to it.

---

[1] Aini is a branch of the Hani Ethnic Group in southernmost Yunnan Province, China

Snake meat is edible, snake skin marketable, and snake bile useable as an ingredient of traditional Chinese medicine.

As soon as he was aware of external events in his childhood, Gebu began to hunt snakes with his father for a living. He had learned all the nitty-gritty skills of tackling snakes...

He could pull a coiling banded krait[2] from a tree by its tail and thrash it like a rope until its spinal bones were separated. He dared to grab a cobra[3] by its expanded neck and strangle it while it was raising the front part of its body to lunge and hiss. Before a loudly vibrating rattlesnake[4] had time to flee, he could clench its tapered mouth close to prevent it from baring venomous fangs.

A snake in the hands of Gebu was as good as in the mouth of a mongoose.

Like the mongoose, Gebu was certainly nonimmune to snake venom.

But it was always impossible for venomous snakes to get hold of him as he attacked like a whirlwind and dodged like lightning.

Even if he was accidentally bitten by a venomous snake, he could always get himself out of danger with the antidotes he had with him all the time.

---

[2] In the Aini vernacular, it is called *jinjiaodai* (golden puttee)

[3] The Aini people call it *fanshaoqian* (beautiful spoon)

[4] The Chinese also call it the "five-step snake," believing that, once bitten, no one can walk five steps away before dying.

Gebu was only twenty-five, but the snakes he had conqu-
ered were enumerable.

He was extremely confident of successfully tackling any
snake.

But this time, the snakes he was going to face caused him
to knit his eyebrows.

These snakes were hard to deal with.

Because they had two legs!

Chapter 3

Two-legged living beings are certainly not serpents. They are humans.

Why did a snake handler had to deal with humans?

Who were they?

They were drug gangs active in the area of Mount Nanla on the southern border of Yunnan Province, China.

Gebu was dispatched by the captain of the provincial anti-drug police to investigate before catching them.

As an investigator, Gebu was not only good at capturing snakes in the subtropical jungle to which he had been accustomed, but he was also an ethnic Aini who found himself in his element when dealing with fellow Aini villagers.

Therefore, he was the best choice for this mission.

The drug dealers of Mount Nanla had long been colluding with those on the other side the border.

Circulating here was a popular doggerel:

There're two pests in Mount Nanla:

Iron's Head does people hurt;

Mountain Wind plays havoc.

"Iron's Head" originally refers to an extremely venomous pit viper species native to the jungle of Mount Nanla. But the doggerel refers to a big drug lord across the border. Not only was he named Zhou Laotie, but his head was also shaped like laotie, meaning "iron" in the sense of a household appliance. His nickname derives from his broad forehead and jutting chin, which bore a resemblance to the head of a pit viper.

Mountain Wind was the nickname that Lao Ba gave to himself. He was a drug lord native to the area. "Mountain Wind" is originally a nickname for cobras, which are exceedingly poisonous. With a ferocious temper, a cobra often grips a person with its fangs relentlessly until he is dead. By giving himself such a scary name, Lao Ba demonstrated what kind of a character he was.

These two vipers had been entrenched in the area of Mount Nanla for years.

None of the gangs wanted to concede defeat to the other in the fight for drug monopoly.

The anti-drug police were determined to eradicate the two vipers, particularly the native Mountain Wind.

Iron's Head was terrified at the news of the crackdown whereas Mountain Wind would not take the prospective eradication lying down.

The two contending vipers began to collude with each other when they found themselves in a life-threatening situation. They were like the natural enemies, a fox and a rat, in a forest, running for their lives together when a rainstorm was imminent.

Without firearms, Mountain Wind found his gang, equipped only with crossbows and pole spears, to be vulnerable to the armed anti-drug police troops who were trying to encircle and annihilate them. He asked well-armed Iron's Head for help. At his request, Iron's Head provided him with firearms in secret in the hope of rejuvenating his own drug business while Mountain Wind was entangled with the anti-drug police in a "guerrilla warfare."

An extremely accidental opportunity enabled the anti-drug police to intercept some guns and ammunition that

Iron's Head was smuggling across the border to Mountain Wind. The police began to discover that the two vipers were working together in stealth.

Nevertheless, the thick jungle and the treacherous terrain, culminated with the scattering nature of the drug dealers, presented great difficulty to the anti-drug campaign to get rid of Mountain Wind.

Iron's head saw this difficulty as an opportunity…

If one smuggling effort failed, he could try it a second time.

The weapons, once fallen into the hands of Mountain Wind, would put him in a better position of fighting against the anti-drug police.

The urgent task before the police was to find out and cut off the secret channel between the two vipers and eventually foil Iron's Head's plot to smuggle the weapons to aid Mountain Wind.

It was easy said than done!

The area of Mount Nanla connects to the border. It is covered with rolling mountains and endless forests. Mountain villages dotting here and there like stars were home to various mingling ethnic peoples.

There are a few dozen paths leading to Mount Nanla from across the border. The residents and merchants from both sides often come and go, either to visit relatives or do business.

Where to begin to find out the secret channel between the two vipers in such a complex situation?

Just at this time, the anti-drug police received a secret letter with a piece of kemu in the envelope.

The letter came from the Caoluo (Falling Grass) Street situated at the northwestern corner of Mount Nanla.

The sender of the letter was Weng Guo, deputy leader of the Police-Civilian Integrated Defense Team (PCIDT).

In the letter, Weng Guo wrote that a horse train carried four loads of goods from across the border. The goods were neither sold at Caoluo Street nor transported out of it. The caravan mysteriously vanished.

Weng Guo suspected that they were not ordinary goods, but firearms. He asked that the anti-drug police contact him as soon as possible.

Firearms?

From across the border again!

This was exactly where the anti-police were anxious to start and had found it hard to do, wasn't it?

This was a very important clue!

Strangely, there was also a piece of kemu with Weng Guo's letter.

The ethnic Aini people do not have their writing system. Since ancient times, they have been recording things or sending messages by wooden or bamboo slips carved with various marks and signs.

Wood or bamboo slips carved in this manner are referred to as kemu, or literally "carved wood." The kemu that Weng Guo sent were 16.65 centimeters long and 3.8 centimeters wide. The sign carved on it was only a shaft of an arrow.

A complete arrow means an announcement of an on-going battle.

A shaft without the arrowhead meant an urgent invitation to a meeting to discuss a warfare. Weng Guo retained the other half of the bamboo kemu with the arrowhead carved on it. The recipient of the letter, after locating Weng Guo, had to present his kemu half to match Weng Guo's. Only when, like a tally, the two halves put together presented seamlessly a whole arrow could Weng Guo trust the recipient of the letter and began to discuss with him matters concerning the battle.

Another significance of using kemu lies in its confidentiality.

It means that situations at the venue of the rendezvous could be so complicated that the liaisons had to conceal their identity to fend off possible plots of assassination.

So, why did Weng Guo take such drastic measures by sending a request for a meeting in an ancient, usual manner?

The map showed that Caoluo Street was on a level ground closest to Mount Nanla. It was also next to the border.

Because of its unique location, the two vipers had chosen it as their secret liaison station.

It was conceivable that situations in such a place were more complicated than those of ordinary places.

After repeated discussions, the anti-drug police came to two conclusions:

Either Weng Guo deliberately played a deceptive trick

like a magician did to use a left-hand move to cover what he really wanted to conjure up in his right hand or he was in such a difficult position that he could not confide his secret to anyone except the dispatch from the anti-drug police.

No matter what the answer to the puzzle was, the anti-drug police had no alternative but to send someone over with the half of the kemu tally.

And, as the headless-arrow message indicated, the dispatch had to go incognito.

The anti-drug police had to assign the mysterious and critical task to Gebu although he had been neither to Caoluo Street before nor acquainted with Weng Guo.

The reason was that most of the residents of Caoluo Street were ethnic Aini people. Gebu was the ideal candidate.

Meanwhile, Kaluo, leader of the PCIDT, was his parallel cousin. Undoubtedly, he could become his right hand.

Gebu set off with the assigned task.

He dressed up as a snake merchant carrying a cloth sack.

Rich businessmen travel either by car where roads accessible or on horseback where they are not.

But cars or horses would invite fellow travelers' attention, making them think of his cloth sack being filled with banknotes.

Gebu was not supposed to attract any attention on his journey.

It would be better if no one paid any attention to his appearance.

Besides, he wanted to take a short cut by surmounting high and precipitous mountains. It would be inconvenient to travel on horseback.

Without further ado, he set out on foot.

People walk on two legs.

Legless, snakes can slither on grass.

The ribs of a snake can move freely. When a snake travels, its ribs are pulled by the muscles between them that contract them one by one, and the contraction ripples from the front to the back to pull the scales on its belly. The scales, in turn, take advantage of the friction of the uneven ground to drag its body forward. To speed up, a snake can also wiggle its body left and right, thus moving in a unique "snaking" manner.

The ribs can contract very fast, and a snake can travel at a lightning speed with the help of its wiggling movement.

To get hold of a snake, the catcher must run faster.

Gebu had learned to move fast through snake hunting.

Therefore, when he walked, he could trot as if he were flying.

Leaving at a starry night, he had traveled twenty-four hours in the mountain.

He encountered no other dangers on his way than a robber trying to attack him.

When the sun he had seen rising again was about to set, Gebu had sneaked out of a pass, only to catch sight of the glinting Nanla River at the foot of the mountain.

Behind the lush trees along the riverbank were rows of houses of uneven heights. That was where Caoluo Street lay.

I'm almost there finally!

Gebu took a deep breath, held his steps, and opened his shirt, allowing the mountain wind to pound his chest like a hammer beating on an anvil.

Beads of sweat streamed down his ruddy face. He did not bother wiping them. Opening his bright eyes wide, he fixed his bright eyes on Caoluo Street at the mountain foot.

He knitted his brows into deep furrows.

What was in store for Red-faced Mongoose?

Would it be a trap?

Or a bush of knives?

Or the fanged mouth of a venomous snake?

"Be cautious! Be careful! Unless it's absolutely necessary, never disclose your identity, even to a relative of yours. Remember, you're a snake merchant. You're going there because of snakes."

Gazing at Caoluo Street, Gebu regurgitated what the company commander of the anti-drug police had told him.

Yes, because of snakes, snakes!

Just then, a horse was heard clip-clopping at the bend of a mountain path.

A man galloped up from the foot of the mountain.

Chapter 4

When the rider came up to him, Gebu could not but feel shocked.

It was a man with a square face, on which there was a nose of prominent bridge and a pair of thin almond eyes beneath caterpillar-like eyebrows. He was wearing a short shirt with its bottom reaching only to the chest; and a pair of loose pants reaching beyond the knees, and a waist band made of leopard skin. He had a curved, Burmese dagger on his waist.

He was a handsome Aini man of valiance.

He was none other than Kaluo!

"Kaluo Aguo[5]!" Gebu blurted out.

With the call, the rider alighted from the horse and landed with a thump.

The thump sounded firm and yet elastic. Gebu noticed that Kaluo were wearing a pair of rubber-soled shoes.

It was a pair of new generation of rubber-soled shoes worn by policemen.

Kaluo fixed his wide-open eyes on Gebu and suddenly put his arms around his shoulders.

"It's you, Gebu?"

His voice quivered somewhat with excitement.

Wow, how familiar the voice was, booming but a bit raspy!

Gebu was also excited. He felt Kaluo's hands on his shoulders as strong as a metal hoop around a barrel.

"Yes, it's me, Bro!"

Time slipped away fast. It had been six years since they last met. Both the parallel cousins had wrinkles added to their foreheads.

Their sudden reunion reminded them of what had happened in the past, which seemed like only yesterday.

"Brother Kaluo, do you still remember?" asked Gebu, his eyes blinking. "That evening six years ago, you fled to our

---

5 "Aguo" is an Aini dialect meaning "brother." So, "Kaluo Aguo" means "Brother Kaluo"

stockage village like a muntjac after you pissed some drug dealers off. You meant to resettle there but the drug dealers were bent on chasing you down and killing you, so you had to flee again. The day you were leaving, I gave you a send-off, and we drank wine mixed with sacrifice blood. You told me, 'There are rocks when there are mountains; there's rain when there're rivers. So long as I'm still alive, we're bound to see each other again!' See, sure enough, we're seeing each other again now."

Rubbing Gebu's shoulders with his hands, Kaluo sighed emotionally, "Yes, after the wind is gone, the trees will stand straight again. Although we had been through trials and tribulations in the past few years, we're still not only alive but also fit and strong. After all, we can see each other again!"

As he said so, Kaluo lifted the cloth sack on Gebu's shoulder a bit.

"Well, you're still living by catching snakes, aren't you?"

"A tree not yet struck down by lightning must continue to live by growing its roots in the ground. How can I support myself without catching snakes?"

"You're right. Gebu, have you married?"

Forcing a smile, Gebu said, "In my line of work, I compare myself to a piece of common duckweed: I stay a few more days where the water is static, and I take to my heels when there's a torrent. I can hardly make my ends meet, so how can I afford to support a family?"

"My good bro, if you find it hard to make a living, come to live with me here."

"Great. A brother is a brother after all. Kaluo, how are you doing?"

"Without a straw raincoat, you're vulnerable to thistles and thorns; without a bamboo hat, you're bound to expose your head to the rain.' I'd traveled here and there, with my scalp almost peeled off by sunshine, until I finally settled down in the mountain behind Caoluo Street. I'm now married with children. One day, I was going to the market to sell some medicinal herbs and mushrooms I'd collected when I saw the locals trying to capture a couple of robbers. I joined them and threw one of the robbers to the ground and trussed him up. Later, the Police-Civilian Integrated Defense Team (PCIDT) was set up and I was elected its leader. While knowing I was flattered, I accepted the position. But as I became busy, I had less time to take care of my family. I haven't seen them for half a year. This afternoon, my wife asked someone to pass me a message that both her and the children got sick and asked me to return and take a look. I'm ready to rush to them in the dark of the night."

"Ahh," Gebu said knitting his brows, "Since both your wife and children are sick, you must hurry and get to them sooner! Is it still far away?"

"No, not too far away. In such bright moonlight, I can get to them as soon as a chicken is cooked. But…"

"But we've got to say goodbye after we're just reunited, right?"

"Yep!"

"Bro, a rabbit's tail is short, but life is long! We've got

enough time to see each other."

"Okay, Gebu. Since you're still a single, you'd better stay in Caoluo Street now that you're here. No matter how high it flies, a hawk must have a nest after all. I'll be back in a couple of days. Let's work together here in Caoluo Street. You can catch snakes and treat people bitten by snakes, so you'll be a great asset to our PCIDT!"

With that, Kaluo mounted his horse.

"Bro, be careful as you travel in the night!"

"Don't worry. I've got used to it. Gebu, when you get to Caoluo Street, you may stay at the PCIDT and tell them you're my parallel cousin."

Gebu said, "'Lips are but two pieces of flesh and produce words when they touch each other.' Mere verbal statement can't be taken as a proof. So, they may not trust me. I may just as well stay in an inn and do my snake business as usual. I'll wait till you return."

Kaluo nodded, "That's a good idea. So, you may have to put up with what you can get for a few days. I'm leaving now. You must wait till I come back."

After he finished, he gave his horse's belly a spur.

Neighing, the horse elevated its neck.

Then, it galloped away clip-clopping.

Watching the horse kicking up dust and disappearing at the end of the mountain path, Gebu felt a heavy sense of loss.

The unforgettable moments of their being together in the past presented themselves to his mind's eye like a movie, frame by frame.

A sense of guilt somehow swelled up in him when he thought of the lies he had told Kaluo. He felt uneasy and sorry. He was his parallel cousin through thick and thin after all.

But what should he have told him? The truth?

Gebu remembered what the company commander of the anti-drug police had told him:

"Don't be emotionally attached to anyone, not even me, because feelings will soften the heart. To a drug investigator, the harder-hearted, the better."

It was hard to understand what the captain had said.

So, we can't even be attached to our comrades, comrades-in-arms, and our loved ones?

Can feelings really soften a man's heart?

Wouldn't people treat each other too callously if they didn't have feelings?

Still pondering, he turned and resumed his journey.

As he approached Caoluo Street, Gebu sneaked into a roadside grove of broad-leaved trees.

When he looked around and found nothing astir, he pulled the handgun from within his shirt, wrapped it up in a piece of oiled paper, and buried it at the base of a big tree.

Then, he marked the spot.

Being unarmed would help conceal his identity as an investigator. Meanwhile, it could also remind him to be cautious all the time.

However, as an old saying goes, "Without coincidences, there would be no stories."

While burying his gun, Gebu only watched for things around him, completely unaware of a pair of wide-open eyes in the thick foliage above him watching his every move.

After concealing his gun, he produced the kemu tally from within his shirt and hid it in the headwear of dark blue cloth that he was wearing.

Now that he was ready, he headed straight for Caoluo Street.

Chapter 5

Caoluo Street at dusk quieted down like bois-terous birds perching in their nests.

Both the stall vendors and marketgoers carr-ying bam-boo baskets on their backs had dispersed before sunset. The street revealed its uneven sur-face paved with pebbles.

The pebble-paved surface was littered with fruit skins, peals, and husks, as well as trampled blobs of donkey and horse dung.

The few eateries had shuttered one after another, so that the hubbub of drinkers' wager game was no longer audible.

Under the royal poinciana tree in the middle of the street, a few people were still crowding around a couple of stalls not yet packed up.

What they were selling must have been seafood and meat, which could go bad overnight. The vendors had to bite the bullet and sold them at prices they reduced repeatedly with great reluctance.

Generally speaking, the main part of a small street like this is where people buy and sell things to eat.

To find places to stay, one had to go to a backstreet.

As he headed toward a backstreet, Gebu was pondering…

The only person who can become my right man is Kaluo, but he is away. So, I must rely on myself for now.

I'll get in contact with Weng Guo as soon as I've found a place to stay.

What kind of a lodging place shall I choose to stay?

Yes, I must find an inn where horse *guotou*[6] were usually staying. Those people travel everywhere and must be the

---

[6] "guotou" is the nickname given to a horse-puller in a horse train or caravan

best-informed. Drinking and eating with them may be of great help to my investigation task because I can listen to them talking with a loose tongue.

Passing by a stall not yet packed up, he suddenly heard someone roaring in the crowd:

"There's no such a thing in the world like cutting down fruit tree to pick its berries! You're such bullies! Their fish are caught with hard labor, not blown over by the wind. They'll be inexpensive when they're given free? I think even if they're given free, you'd still complain about fish bones. Hey, fishmonger bro, as you need money urgently, I'll buy them all. Take the money and see if it's enough to take your sick child to a doctor."

After the roar died down, a bulky, dark-complexioned man squeezed out of the crowd pulling his shoulders back. Carrying four to five black carps in his hand, he pitter-pattered barefoot on the pebble surface of the street.

His weather-beaten face looked swarthy and as coarse as the bark of a tree. Years of padding mountain paths turned the soles of his feet as tough as horse hooves.

He was a long-time traveler in the mountains and on wilderness.

Stunned by the swarthy man's harangue, the few hagglers around the fishmonger's stall were rolling their eyes aggrievedly.

Gebu adjusted his own pace and caught up with the man.

Some of the hagglers grumbled indistinctly:

"You're nothing but a reckless horse-puller! Who can guarantee you'll still be alive tomorrow? Who, living a normal life, would like to compete with you?"

"That's true! What's the point of acting like a gentleman here? Go back to your inn to shoo mosquitoes for your horses."

The grumble was as low as the buzz of mosquitoes.

The buzzes, however, proved Gebu's assessment: this swarthy man was frank and bold and has a strong sense of brotherhood. He was a horse-puller that had traveled far and wide. He and his caravan stayed in one of the lodgings here.

Watching the swarthy man walking away, Gebu was convinced that he could be of great help.

Gebu doubled his steps and caught up with him.

"Bro! Bro!"

Hearing someone calling him from behind, the swarthy man stopped, turned around, and sized Gebu up and down, his black brows flapping like the wings of an eagle.

His piercing eyes told Gebu that he was a vigilant and seasoned caravan horse-puller.

Gebu also held his steps, beaming, embarrassed, and a bit timid.

"So?" asked the swarthy man puzzled, "You want the fish?"

"No, no," Gebu kept shaking his head, "I'm a traveler and I'm new here. I was so touched when I saw you fighting for justice, so I caught up to ask for advice…"

The swarthy man cut him short:

"A bird from the south side of the mountain lands in the forest on the north side. It's now worrying about where to perch, isn't it?"

He is really an old hand that has seen the world!

"Yes, yes!" Gebu nodded like a pecking chicken hen.

"A total stranger and a single, you're looking for a reliable lodge, right?" asked the swarthy man.

"Yes, yes! You're so perceptive that you can read my mind. I live by catching and selling snakes." At this, Gebu relieved himself of the cloth sack containing snake-catching tools. "I'm here at Caoluo Street to learn about the market conditions. If it's good, I'll catch snakes in the mountain and sell them in the market. If not, I'll buy some snakeskin and snake bile and sell them somewhere else."

The swarthy man laughed upon hearing his self-introduction.

"Ha-ha! Either selling the snakes you catch yourself or trading their parts, you're doing a brisk business!"

Gebu said, "With a small capital that yields a meager profit, I'm barely making my ends meet."

The swarthy man said, "Don't worry! I'm not going to rob you. What rich merchant doesn't drive a car or ride a horse? As soon as I saw you hitting the road on foot, I knew you were penniless. You're looking for a safe place to stay not to protect your money, but your life, right?"

"You're right! You're definitely right!"

"Then, come with me to the Loquat Horse Caravan Inn where I'm staying."

Gebu pretended to be surprised, "So? Bro is also staying in the inn?"

"Sure!"

"When I saw you buying fish, I thought you were a local. That's why I asked you for direction."

"Ha-ha!" The swarthy-faced man chuckled and said, "My name's Heize[7], but they all call me Swarthy Guotou (Black Horse-Puller). You can also call me so if you like. My brother and I work in the same horse caravan to transport food and clothing for their owners. We come and go, and each time we pass Caoluo Street, we stay in the Loquat Horse Caravan Inn. It has more people, which means more excitement, and the inn owner Boss Lu is so honest that he never overcharges us. You'll be rest assured that you'll be safe here. But here's a catch: the horses smell. Hope you don't mind."

Gebu burst into a laughter.

---

[7] The Chinese character pronouncing "hei" in the name means "swarthy"

"It's my good luck to stay with you, my Old[8] Bro. I can't be too happy! They say it's good to be at home for a thousand days, and it's difficult to be away from it every minute. I've really run into a good man that I can go to in case of difficulty."

Swarthy Guotou laughed as well.

"Whether I'm good or not is one thing, but it's indeed difficult to be away from home. As a saying goes, 'Just as a sliding rock can be stopped by a tree, a traveler needs the help of fellow travelers.' What kind of a traveler doesn't help others or never needs others' help?"

They chatted as they walked to the depth of the back-street.

Before they reached the end, they turned to a small gravel path that led diagonally away from the back street.

From a distance, a loquat grove came into view, and behind the flickering foliage, there stood rows of houses with mud walls and thatched roofs.

A horse snort or two were heard from time to time.

It went without asking that this must be the Loquat Horse Caravan Inn that Swarthy Guotou had mentioned.

The inn's name must have derived from that lush loquat grove.

---

[8] Old added as a prefix to the name of a person senior in one's age or superior in one's rank is a show of respect in Chinese culture.

Gebu asked, "May I ask how long you'll stay here for this trip, Bro?"

Swarthy Guotou sighed.

"Humph! We meant to stay overnight before we hit the road. But a few of our loads went lopsided and fell into the river when we were crossing it. We have no choice but to spend two more days air-drying the unhusked rice. Otherwise, it'd grow into rice seedlings when we get to our destination, wouldn't it?"

"I see, Bro. So, you're transporting grain on this trip."

"True! We bought the unhusked rice in the seat of the prefecture. The grain is said to be provisions for the garrison troops. They're still waiting, but now we've dampened it. We can't leave until the day after tomorrow at the soonest."

"Well, people only pay attention to the rice but overlook the hardships behind its growth and handling. How many people must work hard before a grain of rice ends up in the mouth."

Gebu appeared to remember something suddenly and continued:

"Bro, I've got a cousin, my father's brother's son. He's also doing rice business on the other side of the border. Not long ago, he asked someone to send me a message, asking me to find out what the formalities he must complete to sell unhusked rice to Caoluo Street."

"It depends on how much grain you sell," replied Swarthy Guotou. "If not much, say two basketfuls carried by a shoulder pole, no one cares. If you're selling a lot, you must contact the PCIDT, or rather, its leader Kaluo... Oh, no, he's just gone. I saw him riding his horse through the street. Then, you have to see the deputy leader Weng Huzi (Beard Weng) and ask him to write you a certificate."

"Beard Weng?"

"His name is Weng Guo. Because he grows a beard and has no time to trim it regularly, people gave him the nickname. Hey, did you see over there?" Swarthy Guotou pointed behind him and went on, "See the big banyan tree over there?"

Gebu looked in the direction he pointed and in the evening twilight, he spotted the huge banyan towering in a grove of trees and a row of houses in the distance.

He nodded.

"Weng Guo's house is right under that banyan tree. He calls it home, but it's more like a store. He's still a single. I mean not married yet."

"Not sure if this deputy leader is nice to talk to."

"Just go to him. His bark is worse than his bite, so to speak. You won't be disappointed. In my opinion, he must have scared all the girls away with his barks and remains a single, as single as a tree."

While chatting, they entered the loquat grove.

Swarthy Guotou pushed a fence gate, and they entered a

yard, only to run into a skinny old man.

Swarthy Guotou greeted him loudly, "Boss Lu!"

Gebu reciprocated his greetings politely.

Fixing his sparkling eyes on Gebu for a while, Boss Lu directed them at Swarthy Guotou and asked,

"This gentleman is…"

Patting Gebu on his shoulder, Swarthy Guotou answered,

"This is a customer I've got you. He's Gebu, a snake merchant."

Gebu bowed to Boss Lu and said,

"A muntjac sweating after traveling has come to the loquat grove to cool itself off in its shade. I'm here to ask for your indulgence!"

Boss Lu laughed his head tilted up,

"Don't stand on ceremony! It's a shame it's been quite some time since we harvested the loquat berries. Otherwise, I could treat you to some of them. Well, I hope I'll be lucky enough to serve you in the long run. If you don't mind my shabby rooms and amenities, I wish you could patronize my shabby inn more often in the future."

"I'm sure I'll come to bother you often," said Gebu while bowing a second time.

Swarthy Guotou burst into a laugh.

"You see, Boss Lu? He is so polite. After all, he's a merchant, not a caravan horse-puller like me." As he finished, he lifted the big batch of black carps in his hand and, shaking them a bit before Boss Lu, said, "I bumped into a fishman friend on the street, and he gave me the fish. Please have your chef to fix a fish dish with them, so it'll go with the wine we'll drink together."

"Great! We don't have to worry about the lack of fish or wine." Then, Boss Lu looked back and shouted into the kitchen:

"Langzhe! Hey, Langzhe!"

With the call, a chubby inn assistant with a round face scurried out of the kitchen.

He might have been building a fire and blowing it with his mouth: his nostrils were smeared with soot.

"Yes, sir, I'm coming!" He responded as he came out running.

"Take the fish in and prepare them. Fix two more meat dishes and serve them together to Swarthy Guotou in his room as supper!" After giving his order to Langzhe, he turned to Gebu,

"Let's go! I'll show you your room!"

Gebu was about to leave when Swarthy Guotou called him:

"Gebu, wine is a relative of a group of people. Come and join us tonight! My brother and I stay in the room on the north side.

Gebu said promptly, "I haven't repaid you for showing me the way here. How can I drink my benefactor's wine? Bro, thank you very much, though! I've just eaten so much and so fast that I'm still feeling stuffed. I've already checked in, so I'd like to go out to walk off the extra food I've eaten. Sorry but I can't drink with you tonight!"

"That's okay. Drop in when you are available. See our room from here? The one where the grain is being air dried."

Gebu had already laid his eyes on the large patch of grain spreading on the ground. He also noticed a row of horseback loads, each having a wide, red cloth ribbon tied to it.

Each of the ribbons was tied firmly into the "hero's knot," in the style of a turban-like headgear worn by some of the minority ethnic groups in Yunnan.

Gebu nodded to Swarthy Guotou and said,

"Uh-hu, I saw the grain, as well as the row of horseback loads with red ribbons tied to them."

"Ha-ha-ha! Those red cloth ribbons are the marks I made to my loads. I don't want them to be mixed with the loads of other caravans because mine contain army provisions."

"Great! I'll come to see you when I'm free."

With that, Gebu went away with Boss Lu.

Gebu meant to ask Boss Lu for a single room to facilitate his investigation task.

But he bit his tongue…

It'd appear more natural if he just did as the host thought fit.

Besides, single rooms were more expensive. Such a request would be unfit for a poor itinerary snake merchant.

To his surprise, Boss Lu seemed to have read his mind and led him through the loquat grove to the east end of the inn and placed him in a single room there.

The room was very small, built next to a large store-room sharing the same gable wall. However, it was kept immaculately tidy and spotlessly clean.

The bamboo bed, stools, and table shone with a brownish gloss. The white mosquito net had been washed pale, and in it a quilt with cotton wadding and small-flower patterns was folded neatly.

His satisfaction with this single room manifested involuntarily in his expression.

Boss Lu blurted out, "Looks like you're okay with this small room."

Gebu stumbled briefly.

"Oh, yes. As my line of work is dealing with snakes, no one would like to see them, dead or alive. I'd better not sharing a room with other guests. Even if they didn't protest publicly, they'd talk behind me. It's hard to find a proper place for a sack of snakes. So, I'm so lucky to have this little room, where I can hit the pillow as soon as I feel sleepy. But what's the damage for a room like..."

"Well," said Boss Lu with a smile, closing his round eyes into bean-sprout-like slits. "I was worrying you might not be happy with a room at the end of the inn so small that you would find it inconvenient to move about. I'm happy so long as you think it's okay. Don't bother the room payment. Ours is the least expensive in Caoluo Street. You pay me if your business on this trip is profitable. If not, you may pay me when you come the next time."

Gebu found Boss Lu's kind words hard to respond.

Before withdrawing himself from the room, Boss Lu said caringly,

"'A bird may prefer nestling, but the wind won't subside.' Doing business away from home, you must be careful all the time. Return to the inn early every evening. You can't roam around in the dark night outside. If you have any need, feel free to see me in my accountant's office. You're a new comer and don't know me much. I used to be a horse-puller myself before, and I'm the most empathetic to travelers."

Gebu heaved a deep sigh of relief after Boss Lu's departure.

He could finally rest after two days of traveling.

But he could not because he had to get in touch with Weng Guo.

Gebu mulled over what Swarthy Guotou had told him about Weng Guo:

His barking is worse than his bite. He is given the nickname Beard Weng because he grows a beard and has no time to trim it.

What secret does Weng Guo have behind the carved message on the kemu tally?

Gebu pushed open the bamboo door and standing on his toes, peered at the soaring banyan tree half hidden in the gathering dusk.

Chapter 6

Under the big banyan tree, there was a court-yard fenced by bamboo stems.

The spaces between the stems were overgrown with cactuses.

The thick, decrepit stems and leaves betrayed the age of the bamboo walls.

A partially adobe old house with a thatched roof took over all most all the space in the small courtyard.

This lonely old house accompanied by the equally lonely banyan tree stood aloof from the other courtyards.

Parts of the mud plaster on the walls began to peel off and the thatched roof had become desiccated and darkened. The whole residence assumed a grim appearance in the dusk.

No one knew what generation owner Weng Guo, a fairly young single, was of the solitary old house.

As Gebu approached the old house slowly, it was deathly quiet around the banyan tree.

The two small windows in the old house stared at Gebu like the dark eye sockets in a skull.

A few aerial roots of varying lengths were hanging down in front of the courtyard gate like a devil's talons.

Whiffs of spooky cold air sneaked out of the shades of the trees.

Gebu deliberately stumped a little as he walked up so that the house owner could hear a visitor approaching.

However, the door was kept ajar, and there was nothing astir behind it.

The two dark windows were still staring like a skull's eye sockets.

There was apparently no on in the house.

It's already evening, why in the world is Weng Guo not back home?

Without hesitation, Gebu went up straight to the gate of the courtyard.

The gate was a bunch of red cedar boards nailed toge-ther.

It was weathered so much that the boards' original bloody red color had been reduced to a brownish hue. A few broad-leaved vines crawled randomly over the gate.

Arriving at the gate, he was wondering whether he should push it open or knock at it when, all of a sudden…

Creak!

The red-cedar gate opened of itself.

Gebu was taken aback.

From the crack of the gate, a face stuck out through the

green vines…

It was a terrifying face!

A deep knife scar furrowed from the top of his forehead down to the upper part of his nasal bridge, thereby pulling one of his caterpillar-like brows higher than the other. A pair of chilling, impassive beams shot out of his big, round eyes like the glint of a blade yanked out of its scabbard.

His big eyes set off the scarred swarthy face, making it look thinner and more like an upside-down ox horn.

Gebu was startled more by the grim expression on the scarred face than by its sudden appearance before him.

On this grim face, his features seemed to freeze. It was like an iron ingot or a dark cloud, a glimpse of which would send a chill down the spine of the beholder.

Gebu felt instinctively that behind its gloom, the face, albeit its impassiveness, revealed a trace of hostility, an aura of death, and an element of elusive secrecy.

If what Swarthy Guotou said about the beard on Weng Guo's face was correct, then this beardless Scarface was evidently not the person whom Gebu was to meet.

Gebu had to make a quick revision to what he had on the tip of his tongue.

But before Gebu began to say something, Scarface suddenly opened the gate a little further.

His lips seemingly immobile, he blurted out a question more dismal than his expression, and it hit Gebu's eardrums loud and clear:

"Whom are you looking for?"

With an expression of apology, Gebu responded:

"Like a bird flying from afar, I've no idea about the weather here. If I'm at the right address, you must be Brother Zhuang Laohan. Are you?"

To Gebu's question, Scarface remained apathetic.

He neither affirmed nor negated the name "Zhuang Laohan" that Gebu had mentioned.

Gebu had to break the silence.

As if he had met an old acquaintance, Gebu smiled friendlier.

"My name is Gebu. I've done snake business with your elder brother Zhuang Laoyao. Well, 'Comparisons are odious.' A horse is no match to a mule. Your bro thinks and acts faster than I do. His business is so prosperous that he's bought land and houses. Even his waist belt is made of silver. Look at me! Dumb and tongue-tied, I'm still so poor that I can afford a good shirt to cover my belly even though my legs are thinned like toothpicks due to frequent travels. I told him that I'd come to Caoluo Street to scrape a living. Then he gave me your address and asked me to see you no matter what. You're street-smart here, so I'm here to beg for your favor!"

Scarface nodded.

"Haven't found a place to stay?"

"A dumb person like me just had a dumb stroke of luck. I've already checked in to Boss Lu's Loquat Horse Caravan Inn. I came to see you before dark. It seems everything's peaceful. How are you doing, Bro?"

Showing no expression whatsoever, Scarface fixed his eyes on Gebu, his gaze revealing an intimidating chill.

"Thank you for your concern! Zhuang Laohan is not my name. I don't have an elder brother, either."

"What?" Gebu widened his eyes in astonishment and began to stutter, "You...you're not...? Here's the big banyan tree, isn't it? So, I remember the wrong address?"

Scarface fell silent.

"Hmm," Gebu was so embarrassed that he was at a loss what to say, "I'm terribly sorry, Bro, but may I ask if you've been living in this old house all the time?"

Scarface responded coldly, "What else can I help you?"

"I don't think I've anything else. Could you please help me find out if there is a Zhuang Laohan in your neighborhood? His brother asked me to bring him some snake venom antidote. I must live up to our friendship by delivering it to him in person."

"Ahh, if I find him, I'll make sure he'll go and see you at the Loquat Horse Caravan Inn."

What a slick guy Scarface is! With a few words, he's just deprived me of the chance to ask for a second visit.

"A dumb person is indeed blessed with a dumb stroke of luck. I thank you, Bro, on behalf of Zhuang Laoyao."

After he finished, Gebu bowed to Scarface and in the direction where he had come.

He did not look back.

But he did not hear the red-cedar gate close even though

he had covered quite a distance.

Scarface had been gazing at Gebu.

Just as he had been gazing at him from behind the gate, watching him walking up.

He seemed to be expecting someone or doing something evil in secret.

It was certain that Scarface would not have stuck his face out if Gebu had not reached to push the door open.

Who's this Scarface?

Why is he entrenched in Weng Guo's courtyard?

Did Swarthy Guotou give me the wrong address?

While pondering, Gebu turned into a branch path.

He walked further and further, but the Scarface's expression flickered in front of his mind's eye all along.

Although Gebu did not know who he was, Scarface's calmness, alertness, and secretiveness were an indication that he was no ordinary person, and he had something unusual weighing on his mind.

He was walking deep in thought when suddenly something flashed in front of him.

He looked up only to see a startling scene unfolding before his eyes…

A king cobra with the length of a shoulder pole was pouncing on a boy!

The boy was in his early teens, tall but skinny.

The king cobra erected the front quarters of its body like an iron rod and appeared extremely ferocious.

King cobras are the most venomous of all snakes.

Although called "king cobra," it does not have cobra-like markings, that is, the white, eyeglasses-like patterns, on the back of its neck. But it strikes a person in the same manner: raising the front part of its body, extends its hood, and hisses loudly. It is its huge stature and fierce temperament that earn it the royal-sounding name.

Dealing with snakes all year round, Gebu was fully aware of the three particular strengths possessed by the king cobra:

First, not to be startled by the stir of grass, it attacks people preemptively and holds on to its bitten victim.

Second, it is extraordinarily venomous and kills a person in three minutes.

Third, it can squirt venom from its mouth. This is the king cobra's unique tactic of offense. When it launches its attach, it abruptly raises its head a couple of steps away from its victim, and jets his poisonous fluid into his eyes and blinds him instantly.

Because of the three strengths, Gebu was especially cautious whenever he encountered a king cobra.

At this moment, the king cobra was extending its hood and hissed sharply at the boy.

However, the boy was not afraid. Facing the king cobra, he held his machete high ready to meet its challenge.

Seeing the king cobra retract its forked tongue suddenly, Gebu was desperate…

It was a signal that the viper was ready to squirt its venom.

He screamed:

"Jump aside!"

With his scream, he tore his black shirt off, darted forward with a single stride, and cast it out like a fishing net with a whoosh.

The black shirt flew swooshing upon the head of the king cobra like a black cloud. At the same time, the cobra shot out a jet of transparent venom as fast as a fleet arrow, and, with a splash, hit the shirt.

A large patch of the shirt became wet immediately.

Before the king cobra had time to shake the shirt off, Gebu had already gotten hold of it with lightning speed.

He held the king cobra's neck tight while placing a foot on its tail.

Pressing the tail with the foot, he immediately pulled the king cobra's body as straight as a rod.

Unwilling to give in, the king cobra wiggled its body trying to free its tail so that it could entangle Gebu with it.

But, Gebu's grip would not allow it to struggle free.

With supernatural strength summoned in his foot, Gebu nailed its tail to the ground.

Unable to wiggle its tail free, the king cobra instantly changed its strategy. It began to twist its neck desperately and, showing its venomous barbed fangs, turned to bite Gebu's hand.

Like a pair of pliers, Gebu's big hands pinched the neck of the king cobra tight.

These pliers clenched the right spot, that is, the expanded

hood, to prevent it from turning its head around or bending it down.

The wrathful king cobra opened its mouth wide toward the sky, panting heavily.

Drops of venom oozed from the tips of its poisonous fangs.

With all his might, Gebu pulled the king cobra's body tight between his hand and foot.

The king cobra was so angry and frustrated at not being able to exert its strength that it puffed the middle part of its body into a bloated meat balloon.

Like an iron ball, the meat balloon now slid up to its neck trying to knock Gebu's hand, now dropped to its tail with an attempt to crush his foot.

After all the efforts to fight back failed, the king cobra gradually ran out of steam, its body originally as tough as an iron rod now rendered as soft as a rope. White foams gurgled from its fanged mouth as from that of a crab out of water.

Only then did Gebu have the opportunity to train his eyes on the boy.

He had a broad forehead; a jutting chin; a pair of big, dark eyes twinkling like stars; and a tenuous nasal bridge— all arranged properly on his tanned face. Biting his slightly thick lips, he suggested his unbending personality.

Shaking the king cobra in his hand, Gebu said with a smile, "Like it?"

"Yep!"

"Not afraid of it?"

"Nope!"

"You thought you could cut off its head with a swoop of your machete, didn't you?"

"Yes, but I wanted to capture it alive. I just wanted to knock it out with the back my machete."

Gebu immediately took a liking to the boy because of his brief and quick answers.

"But did you notice the wet spot on my black cloth shirt? It's the venom the king cobra squirted. The cobra could've blinded you before you had reached it with your machete."

"I didn't know he had such a trick up its sleeve!"

"Since you like snakes, you're supposed to know all their tricks."

As he spoke, Gebu lifted the front of his shirt, took out a small leather box from his waist, and produced a specially crafted small hook from it. Pointing at the king cobra's two poisonous fangs, he said,

"Look the pair of its fangs, each has a hollow in its middle, like two bamboo tubes. When they bite you, venom will squirt from the tubes. Now, after I pull them out, the cobra won't be deadly anymore."

As he spoke, he extracted the fangs with the small hook.

The boy went to cut a section of a bamboo and came back with it. Gebu then put the king cobra into the tube, sealed both ends, and handed it back to the boy.

"It's yours."

"I can't have it."

"How about me asking you a question? If you can't answer it, you must accept the cobra so that you can study it at home. Would that be okay with you?"

"Hmmm…okay!"

"Now tell me. How did the cobra know you were coming under the tree?"

"It saw me."

"Not a correct answer."

"It smelled me."

"Not either."

"Then…it heard me."

"Still not correct."

"Then, you tell me why."

"King cobras can't see even though they have eyes. Neither do they have noses nor ears. So, they can't see you. Nor can they smell or hear you."

"Then, how did it know I was coming?"

"Stretching out and drawing back, king cobra's tongue works as the nose and the ears in order to detect smell and sound. Besides, did you notice the two small holes by its mouth? They are its most powerful weapons because they can sense temperature. When you walk by, the two holes can detect the heat your body emits, and the king cobra becomes aware of your exact location."

"Wow, how come you know so much?"

"According to what we agreed upon, you must accept

the snake first. Then, I'll tell you how."

"Okay, I accept it," said the boy, who took the bamboo tube with the king cobra in it.

"Child, like you, I've been fond of snakes since childhood. Later, I began to live by catching and selling snakes. Like a leaf being blown by the wind, I do snake business wherever I found myself. Now, I've floated to Caoluo Street as a total stranger." Pointing at the big banyan tree in the distance, Gebu went on, "Look, according to my friend Zhuang Laoyao, his younger brother lives there, but when I asked, I was told that his younger brother isn't living there. The resident is someone whose name is…is…something like Bear Weng…"

"Not Bear Weng. It's Beard Weng," the boy corrected him. "That's Weng Guo!"

"Weng Guo is alright, but why is he called Beard Weng?"

"Because he grows a big beard."

"See, now you know more than I do. Child, what's your name?"

Fixing his big eyes on Gebu, the boy replied,

"If I tell you my name, do you think believe it's real?"

Gebu was shocked but briefly, and he said smiling, "I trust that you won't fool me."

The boy said, "Maybe I will. You'd better not ask anymore."

"So? Why?"

"We're not friends!" said the boy. he turned and ran away, holding the bamboo tube in his arms.

Gebu did not expect boy should reject his effort to befriend him.

Why?

He had just enjoyed a great conversation with him, but now, all of a sudden, he was plunged into an ice house.

The illogical ending suggested vaguely to Gebu that the boy's appearance was by no means accidental.

But Gebu could not tell why on earth it was not accidental at the moment.

He had learned something anyway.

Without realizing it, the boy unwittingly confirmed what Swarthy Guotou had told him…

Weng Guo was indeed the resident of the old house under the big banyan tree.

And he grew a big beard.

It was evening but Weng Guo was not home yet.

He should be home after dark, shouldn't he?

Even though he won't return home after dark, then shouldn't he be home at midnight?

Okay, I'll go to see him at midnight!

Chapter 7

It was midnight.

A man in black sped in the pitch-dark shadows of the trees.

He was wearing a black headwear, black pants, black puttees, and black cloth shoes.

He walked so quietly that his footfalls were inaudible.

Prancing from one tree shadow to another as agilely as a bird gliding into a tree or a fish diving into a pond.

The nightcrawler appeared black all over except his face.

And on his face, there was a beard.

But the bushy facial beard was fake.

The nightcrawler was no one else but Gebu.

Wearing a fake facial beard and dressed in black, he became a different man.

Gebu was so disguised because he had his considerations:

First, before knowing who Weng Guo really was, he would not want him to see his face so that he could have enough room for maneuvers.

Second, with the disguise, he could avoid being recognized by people who had seen him before, including Scarface and that anonymous boy. No matter what, he had revealed his intense interest in Weng Guo and his residence to this intergenerational pair.

Bounding from one tree shadow to another, the nightcrawler Gebu blended himself with the shadows.

He managed to sneak to the big banyan tree and hid behind an aerial root. There, he strained his ears to listen.

He heard nothing but silence.

There was no sound came from the old house, either.

Only a few cricket chirped occasionally.

The solitude in the courtyard was emphasized by the monotonous chirping.

Gebu broke a twig from the tree and tossed it into the yard.

The twig flew tumbling in and fell to the ground with a flop.

The cricket stopped chirping abruptly.

Gebu pricked his ears up.

Profound silence prevailed in the courtyard.

The old house seemed to be in a slumber.

The crickets started chirping again.

The aerial root behind which Gebu was hiding hung from the tree all the way to the ground and into the soil.

This old banyan tree had enumerable aerial roots hanging down from its boughs and branch forks. Some of them ran into the ground while others hung in the air. The latter sucked moisture from the air to nurture their continuous growth until they, too, found their way into the soil below.

An idea dawned upon Gebu.

With a bound, he grabbed an aerial root and quickly pulled himself up to the tree.

He then crawled on his stomach along an old bough that extended into the courtyard. Then, holding an aerial root hanging from the bough, he slid down. The end of the root was dangling a man's height from the ground. He released his grip and jumped to the ground. When he landed, only his toes touched the ground like a butterfly alighting lightly on a blossom. The crickets' serenade was not interrupted.

As soon as he touched ground, Gebu immediately placed his back against the wall.

He saw a window in the wall of the house. He pushed it gently, and it opened ajar.

Yikes! The window was not bolted!

Giving the window another gentle push with his fingers, it was half open.

Just then, Gebu heard a strange scream.

"Boo…"

It was faint and dismal.

It seemed to be coming from either the distant mountains or the room behind the half-open window.

In a deathly quiet night when one could even hear one's own heartbeat, this eerie cry gave one goosebumps.

Gebu's heart jumped a beat. He immediately stopped moving and crouched down, pricking up his ears to listen.

But after only one eerie cry, it was heard no more.

Silence prevailed again.

In the moonlight flooding into the window, Gebu found the room barely furnished. There was only a bamboo table and a stool, as well as a few pots and jars and other miscellaneous articles of daily necessity. There was no bed, so it did not appear to be a bedroom.

He was still puzzled when he suddenly spotted a wooden ladder behind the closed door, and it was only wide enough to allow two feet standing on its rungs.

Gebu came to a sudden realization…

As low as it was, the old house had two stories.

Apparently, Weng Guo slept on the second floor.

In a flash, Gebu hopped into the room through the window and groped toward the door.

He reached to pull back the bolt, but, to his surprise, the closed door was not bolted at all.

Just then, Gebu heard the eerie cry again:

"Boo…"

He gave a shudder, while his hair stood on end.

This horrendous cry was so faint and dismal.

It was so far away, like the howl of a wolf coming from a distant mountain.

Aging, it sounded very close, as if coming right from behind the door or the dark room upstairs.

What's the cry?

His hand still on the bolt, Gebu remained motionless.

He listened for a while, trying to identify the source. But it was quiet again.

Was is a mere acoustic illusion?

Gebu rubbed his ears.

It was not. He was certain that he had heard the ghostly cry.

But he could not tell what gave the cry and where it did it.

Why did this eerie cry sound always appear whenever he made a move?

He heard it when he pushed the window.

He heard it again when he touched the bolt of the door.

It was gone when he calmed down.

Gebu really could not tell if he had heard any strange sound at all.

He fixed his eyes first on the bolt and then on the second floor in the dark.

He gazed at them for a long time but heard nothing astir.

He shook his head and felt the bolt again.

The door was not bolted indeed.

Sleeping while leaving the window open and the door unbolted, why is Weng Guo so careless?

Is he still not home?

Why was he still outside at such a time of night?

He was pondering when suddenly he heard hasty footsteps coming from the woo-den ladder.

Thud!

Thud!

Thud!

Cold sweat broke out on Gebu's forehead. It was too late to conceal himself.

Besides, the room was almost vacant and offered no hideout.

Thud!

Thud!

Thud!

The footsteps were coming toward him.

Focusing his eyes on the wooden ladder, Gebu pressed his hand on the handle of the knife on his waist.

Thud! Thud! Coming down the stairs was but a big rat!

The rat was as big as a weasel.

The rungs of the ladder were sparsely spaced. So, when the rat leapt down, it put a lot of weight on the rungs, thereby making the thudding sound.

As it leapt off the wooden ladder, the rat crawled over his feet without the sligh-test fear.

It either had a poor eyesight or dreaded no people at all.

Chuckling silently, he tiptoed to the second floor arching his back.

Without windows, he could see nothing.

He stood still for a long time to accustomate himself to the darkness. He was even-tually able to see and found a bamboo bed in the corner, covered by a gauze mosquito net.

He tiptoed tentatively a step forward.

As his eyes gradually adjusted to the darkness, he could see a man sleeping on his side in the mosquito net.

It must be Weng Guo.

In his mind's eye, he already saw how Weng Guo was startled awake from his sound sleep.

Well, I'd better push him gently to wake him up naturally.

Gebu went over, gingerly lifted the mosquito net, and

gave the sleeping man a light push on his shoulder.

Weng Guo was sleeping so heavily that he did awaken.

Gebu felt his hand wet. It felt like Weng Guo's perspiration.

He pushed him harder and called in a hushed voice,

"Weng Guo! Weng Guo!"

He was still fast asleep.

Sleeping like a baby, he must have been exhausted during the way.

As he speculated, he came close to see if the sleeping man had a beard.

Suddenly…

A whiff of pungent metallic smell assailed his nostrils.

The smell gave him a shudder, sending a chill down his spine.

He looked close at his hand. Gosh! It was blood!

His hand was covered with blood.

Gebu barely screamed.

Lying in bed was a blood-soaked body instead of a sleeping man.

Gebu's heart pounded hard and fast.

Just then…

Squeak!

It came from the red-cedar gate to the courtyard.

The squeak sounded as if something were being torn. It was jarring and frightening in this silent night.

The crickets around the corner of the wall shut up immediately.

Soon afterwards, people were heard coming.

Thump, thump, thump…

They came straight to the old house.

While they walked quietly, Gebu could still hear them distinctively.

Two people entered the courtyard.

What shall I do?

The door to the old house was not bolted, so the two uninvited visitors were about to burst in.

Why are they walking so quietly? Who are they?

Gebu had no time to ponder because the two guys were about to block him in.

Schwing!

He yanked the knife from its scabbard and climbed down the wooden ladder hurriedly and yet quietly with only his toes touching the rungs as if they were dragonflies dipping their tails in the water.

He found it impossible to jump out of the window. Neither was it possible for him to hide in the barely empty room.

The only option was to lift the big jar from the floor, place it on the wooden trunk, and conceal himself behind them for a little while.

But time would not allow him to do so.

Besides, the jar, if filled with preserved vegetables or

rice wine, would be extremely heavy, thereby giving off some noise when it was placed on the trunk to alert the intruders.

Gebu grew anxious. Meanwhile, the footsteps also reached the door to the old house.

With a squeak, the wooden door was pushed open.

Fortunately, the door was pushed so hard that one of the panels was flung back with Gebu behind it.

Gebu withdraw his chest and abdomen and pressed his back against the wall. Holding his breath, he "disappeared" behind the door.

It was a narrow escape.

If the intruders closed the door behind them, they would see Gebu face to face.

Holding his sharp knife, Gebu was prepared to attack.

With the door being pushed open, moonlight sneaked into the old room and spread on the uneven brick floor, illuminating an oblong spot. Then, a dark shadow of a man appeared in the spot of light as if being projected onto a screen.

Gebu fixed his eyes on the figure in the moonlight.

Suddenly, he saw two prongs sticking out of his head.

Gosh! They seemed to be horns!

Gebu could not believe his eyes.

He looked closely, only to catch a terrifying sight…

The dark figure walking into the moonlight had two horns jutting from his head. He was covered with long hair all over. While he was groping forward, his fumbling hands had nails more than a third of a meter long.

Gebu broke out in a cold sweat.

It can't be a human being?

It's a hairy devil told in fairytales, isn't it?

Holding his knife tight, Gebu kept still gaping at the "hairy devil" in the moonlight.

Only when the "hairy devil" entered did Gebu realize that he was man in a black sheepskin.

The two horns were nothing but bamboo tubes, and each of his fingers had a bamboo slip sharpened at the end attached to it.

Following him was man disguised as a devil.

As soon as they entered, the two "hairy devils" went upstairs.

Luckily, they did not close the door.

They did not expect that there should be eyes watching them behind the door.

The "hairy devil" had an empty gunny sack in his hand.

It seemed that they knew where to go.

It was certain that they came to remove the corpse.

By dressing up as cannibals, they were trying to cover themselves.

They could scare whoever they should bump into on their way out of their wits.

Just then, Gebu heard the bamboo bed creaking.

They're pulling the gunny sack over the body.

Their arrival to remove the body indicates they must have something to do with the victim.

Even if they didn't kill him, they must know the killer!

I must tail them and see where they carry the body.

And see who they're going to contact.

I must also figure out if the victim was Weng Guo.

Making up his mind, Gebu pricked his ears up to listen. Hearing nothing astir outside, he sneaked out of the old house nimbly.

It was chilly outside.

Only then did he realize that he was sweating all over.

He stole out of the small courtyard under the cover of the tree shadow and hid behind the banyan tree.

After quite a while, he heard footsteps coming from the courtyard.

The two "hairy devils" toddled out of the courtyard gate carrying the body.

All of a sudden…

"Boo…"

Gebu heard the eerie cry again.

It was as horrific as dismal.

The cry came from the "hairy devil" staggering behind the other one.

He was mimicking a devil's shriek!

Obviously, he was doing so to whistle in the dark rather than to scare others.

Gebu was about to tag after them when a sinister blast of air caught him from behind.

Before he turned around, a coir rope lassoed his neck.

Gebu tried to grab it in a haste.

But it was still too late.

The coir lasso was tightened around his throat.

Without the chance for an utterance, he began to see the big banyan tree rotating in the moonlight...

Chapter 8

Gebu suddenly heard water tumbling loudly after no one knew how long he had been unconscious during the rotation.

Splashing, splashing! Splashing, splashing!

Soon afterwards, he felt himself being carried forward by his hands and feet.

The ground seemed uneven, as he felt himself bouncing up and down.

The bumpiness shook him completely out of the stupor that he had been going into and coming out of.

The resonant torrent reminded him of a river.

Soon, he felt his face being brushed by gusts of wind, moist, chilly, and slightly fishy.

Ahh, river! Nanla River!

When traveling on the mountain path leading to Caoluo Street, Gebu had seen this glistening river.

Since Caoluo Street was not far from the river, I must be somewhere in the vicinity of Caoluo Street right now.

Gebu did not open his eyes, still pretending to be in the state of unconsciousness.

He could feel that his carriers were trudging on the dry riverbed.

Due to drought, the water of the originally wide river receded to the center of the course, exposing the lateral parts of its riverbed covered with moss-covered rocks and stones.

The rocks could be as large as lying buffaloes whereas the stones could be as small as fists.

Gebu tried to distinguish the footfalls. Suddenly, he realized that apart from the two carriers, there was a third person!

The third person had been walking quietly behind them.

If the carriers are the "hairy devils," then the third person must be the one that attacked me with the coir rope.

After being successful in a sneak attack and sparing my life, he must be harboring a plan.

He was feeling excruciating pain in his neck with the ligature mark left by the coir rope, as if enumerable needles were stuck into it.

He regretted paying all the attention to the "devils" while neglecting what was happening behind him.

Three people traveling in two teams, one must cover the other by walking either in the front or at the rear.

The tactic was not too smart, but why did I lose my vigilance?

I'm now in grave danger in the hands of the three gangsters.

Who are they?

What are they going to do with me?

There're too many questions to answer, but what's critical right now is find a way to escape!

He was pondering when one of the gangsters said,

"Let's dump this beard man here!"

The voice was booming and somber.

It was the voice of the man tagging after them.

Gebu was satisfied with the epithet "beard man" he gave him, knowing that his disguise was effective.

Hearing the gangster who had spoken walking up to him, Gebu desired to see what he looked like.

No, I can't! The moonlight is so bright that I would betray myself if I open my eyes.

Gebu suppressed his urge and kept his eyes closed.

The two men who carried Gebu held their steps and laid him on the ground.

Gebu's back was being dug by the scratchy pebbles.

The moonlight that he had seen through his closed eyelids was gone.

It meant that he was placed in the shade of a big rock.

Gebu stretched his hands and feet a bit in secret.

They were free.

He heard the booming and somber voice again,

"You guys watch him. I'm going to report to Green Bamboo Viper."

What?

Green Bamboo Viper?

Reporting to Green Bamboo Viper?

Gebu heard it clearly.

An old-timer snake handler, Gebu knew everything about green bamboo vipers.

A green bamboo viper is over a third of a meter long with a triangular head, blood-red eyes, and a bamboo-green colored body, on top of which there is a ridge. The tip of the abruptly tapered tail is fiery red. Both nocturnal and diurnal, green bamboo vipers choose to live in shady and damp mountainous areas. Their tails have a strong wrapping power, and they are good tree climbers. Venomous as they are, they excrete very small amount each time, not enough to kill people. But its bite on the head, face or neck is unequivocally fatal.

Green bamboo vipers are best known for being invisible in their camouflage.

They often lie quietly in a bamboo forest, blending their green bodies with equally green bamboo leaves.

Being experts in camouflaging is their important guarantee of getting food and evading their natural enemies.

The "Green Bamboo Viber" mentioned by the gangster must be someone's nickname.

Someone that could decide Gebu's fate.

So, who is he?

Which bamboo forest is he hiding in under the cover of the crisp green color?

There's an Iron's Head across the border and a Mountain Wind on this side. Now, a Green Bamboo Viper has emerged!

Is it an accident for all the vipers to come together?

Crunch, crunch…

The gangster who had volunteered to report to Green Bamboo Viper trudged into the distance on the pebbles.

Lying in the shade, Gebu opened his eyes in slits and saw the back of a skinny and lanky man, who was staggering on the dry peddle riverbed whitewashed by the moonlight.

Suddenly, Gebu felt the skinny and lanky figure facing away was familiar.

Where did I see him?

Ah…

Isn't he Scarface!

The one I saw at the gate of Weng Guo's house!

Is it he?

If so, he must be the killer!

Maybe he had just committed the killing when I caught him ready to leave.

His sullen and unruffled face was one of a killer who would cut down his victims like blades of grass.

Scarface had the time and opportunity to kill.

Then, what was his motive?

Killing someone at dusk and moving the body at midnight—everything seemed to be arranged carefully and planned meticulously.

"Dump the beard man here!"

"You guys watch him! I'll report to Green Bamboo Viper!"

Watching him walking away, Gebu recalled what he had said. The voice, in its natural state, was normal, fluent, and unaffected.

It was a far cry from that of Scarface!

There was a big difference between the two voices despite their equally dismal tone.

So, this acoustic analysis seemed to conclude that it came from a different person…

While contemplating, Gebu stole a brief look at the two gangster carriers.

He saw the four horns swaying in the moonlight.

The carriers were none other than the "hairy devils."

They were now sitting against a rock.

The taller "hairy devil" sat facing Gebu while the shorter one peered at the bank from time to time.

The staggering skinny and lanky gangster had disappeared, leaving only the two "hairy devils" behind.

I must seize the opportunity!

If I let this opportunity slip away, I'd be in bigger trouble when Green Bamboo Viper shows up.

Gebu kept an eye on the "hairy devils" in secret...

Before the attack, he had to figure out what weapons were in their possession.

Splashing, splashing! Splashing, splashing!

The river rushed along.

Its torrent was deafening.

The two "hairy devils" sat motionless on the rock.

They had removed the sharpened bamboo slips from their fingers so that their hands are free to use weapons.

What weapons are they using?

How to expose their weapons?

To scare them by doing a summersault?

Then, Gebu instantly gave up the idea, thinking:

A summersault might be startling enough for his opponents to reveal their weapons, but the move could draw too much of their attention to him and thereby hinder his action.

No, I can't do that. I must make them believe that I'm completely harmless.

So, what shall I do?

Barehanded and not knowing what weapons they've got, I may lose the fight with them.

But time is hard pressed.

He was being secretly anxious when the short gangster said,

"Well, what's the point of reporting? If I were him, I would do something like cleaving a bamboo with a machete: quick and clean. We can just pound him to a meat pie with the stones and rocks available here."

The tall gangster said, "We'd better listen to Green Bamboo Viper. He often warns us that the world is complicated; even a river snail has three spirals!"

The tall gangster spoke while detaching the horns from his head.

The short one fell silent.

Soon, he began to grumble again:

"Looks like we can't have a good sleep. After carrying away a dead body, now we ran into a living one."

Before he finished, a loud sound came abruptly from the river course and disturbed the rhythm of the flowing water.

The sound came from the river.

"Who's it?"

The tall gangster yelled, sprang up, and produced something from his shirt.

He was left handed.

Gebu saw him pulling out a Canadian Mauser C96!

The short gangster also yanking a handgun from his waist.

They both have guns!

Gebu's heart jumped a beat.

He shuddered not at the guns but at what they reminded him of, namely the weapons Iron's Head was smuggling to Mountain Wind and his investigation task on this trip.

The fact that both the gangsters had guns indicated that they came from a usual background.

Gebu picked up a stone larger than a baseball.

With the sturdy stone in his mighty hand, he could smash the brains out of their heads.

Suddenly, another loud sound came from the river.

Instantly, with a flapping sound, a greyish human calf was cast onto the dry riverbed.

The gangsters shrieked with a start.

But soon they discovered that what had been flung to the dry riverbed was not a human calf. It was a fish.

A big black carp as thick as a human calf!

It had swum into a shallow stream and meant to leap back to the deep river. Instead, it unexpectedly crashed on the pebbles as soon as it left the water.

Lying on the pebbles, the whitish fish in the moonlight was tantalizing.

In no time, it started struggling, curving up its head and tail, creating a lot of flap-ping noise.

"Wow!" The short gangster was beside himself with joy, "We aren't staying up for nothing after all! This guy weighs twenty-five kilograms at least."

As he shouted, he put his gun back on his waist and rushed to the big black carp.

The carp had flittered to the edge of the river and was about to flip into it.

The short gangster lost no time in pouncing on it and held it in his arms.

He did not expect that the fish slapped him on his face with its tail.

"Ouch!"

The screaming short gangster fell splashing on his bottom in the water, his hand still gripping the black carp.

Unwilling to give in, the black carp kept flapping its tail.

"Ow! Ouch!"

The short gangster kept screaming.

"Thinking of cooking it into a dish, eh?" boomed the tall gangster, "Mind you! Don't let it eat you first!"

While jeering, he gave Gebu a good kick.

Gebu remained irresponsive.

Seeing this, the tall gangster tucked his gun in his shirt and hurried to help the short one.

As soon as he saw the tall gangster bend down to scoop

the fish, Gebu sprang up, rock in his hand, like a hawk taking off. He then swooped upon the tall gangster from behind.

Gebu planned to take the tall gangster out first.

This thug was burly with broad shoulders. Sandwiched between Gebu and his short accomplice, he shielded the latter's view.

After getting rid of him, Gebu would capture the short one alive so that he could get answers from him to all his questions. Then, he would still have time to deal with him.

But before Gebu could get close, the tall gangster suddenly looked back, and his leopard-like eyes shot out a glare as chilling as the glint of a blade in the moonlight.

Gebu was stunned.

While turning around, the tall gangster pulled out his handgun.

This left-handed thug was really quick with his hand.

In such a situation, a fight to the death was the only option.

A second's delay would prove fatal.

"Charge!"

With a battle cry, Gebu threw himself upon the tall gangster, holding the rock above his head.

The tall gangster refused to buckle. Aiming at Gebu, he pulled the trigger.

He was to put the bullet through Gebu's heart.

The time the tall gangster opened fire, Gebu cast out the rock at him.

Whoosh…

The rock flew toward the muzzle of the gun.

Bang!

The shot was fired.

With a streak of fiery light, there came a smack.

The bullet hit the rock.

The baseball-sized rock was broken into pieces, sending stone pellets in all directions.

Not allowing the tall gangster to fire a second shot, Gebu plunged himself right in front of him. With both his hands, Gebu grabbing the wrist of his left hand that held the gun and hoisted it up into the air…

Bang!

Another shot!

The bullet darted into the night sky.

While lifting the gun up with both hands, Gebu exposed his rib cage.

In a physical fight, one must protect the rib cage where the vital organs like the heart and lungs are contained.

Especially in a close combat, each combatant can hit the opponent's heart in the left part of the rib cage.

In a rush to lift the gun, Gebu made the mistake of over-concentrating on one thing while neglecting the other.

The tall gangster was left-handed. While his left hand was hoisted up in the air by Gebu, his right hand could hit him where his heart was.

Fully aware of this opportunity, the thug kept his gun-holding left hand in the air to prevent Gebu from putting his hands down. Meanwhile, he balled his right hand into a fist as strong as a hammer. He first raised it and then whammed it down forcefully upon the left side of Gebu's rib cage.

Such a knockout punch could crack a rock.

The punch landed right in the Gebu's pit of the stomach.

"Ow!" Gebu gave a heartrending scream. Suffering from sharp pain and short breath, he could hardly stand straight…

But, clenching his teeth, he held his ground.

He could not fall.

If he did, the tall gangster would dig his gun into his back.

Gebu's scream jolted the stupefied short gangster out of his frozen state.

Letting go the big black carp, he picked himself up abruptly and whoosh-pulled his gun out.

The tall gangster was pinning Gebu with his back so that the latter could not move.

The short gangster reached to push the tall one.

In a desperate test of strength with Gebu, the tall gangster erected his back as straight and immobile as a precipitous crag.

Unable to move the tall gangster with his push, the short guy walked around to his side.

At the moment, the tall gangster had just retracted his right hand when he found Gebu still standing.

Punches are not to be wasted.

Retracting a punch might happen in a blink of an eye, but the tall gangster made good use of the fleeting moment to pump a lot of strength into it until all the joints of his finger bones crackled.

When retracted, fist had become harder than a hammer.

The tall gangster swept his punch up from below and hit Gebu with a punch anew right at the pit of his stomach.

This punch hurdled up with the ferocity of a tiger was ten times deadly than the first strike.

Having been hit once and still suffering the pain, how was Gebu able to take this ferocious punch?

Of course, he wasn't.

But, once hit, a lesson learned. Gebu would not allow the thug to strike him a second time.

Before the punch reached him, Gebu had brought his right knee up swiftly, and now he delivered a fierce straight knee strike at the lower abdomen of the tall gangster.

This strike was by no means trivial.

In a fight, there is no need for too many strikes. What counts is a brutal few.

When Gebu had hoisted the tall gangster's gun-holding hand up in the air, he put himself and the thug in a close combat situation.

In a close combat, the two opponents are so near to each other that they cannot hurt by kicking. Instead, they can only fight with their hands, elbows, and knees.

Close to each other, all the vulnerable body locations were soft.

Therefore, during the combat, elbowing and kneeing are more effective than punching.

In an attempt to deliver another punch to Gebu, the tall gangster failed to heed this knee strike to his lower abdomen, a strike with explosive power unleashed from below like "an iron hammer pounding soft meat." How could he stand such a hit?

With a loud "Ow," the tall gangster bent over forward.

Bending over, he had to hang his head down a bit.

Gebu took the opportunity and bumped his head hard into the tall gangster's forehead.

Wham!

His head hit him in the area between his eyebrows.

It is to be noted that Gebu had practiced kung fu in the police with his head bumping into sandbags, tree trunks, as well as bricks and rocks.

Without the training, he would not dare to risk bumping his head in an offensive attack.

This bumping-strike dealt a heavy blow to the tall gangster, sending him seeing stars and caused his head to swim as if he were lost in dense fog and heavy clouds.

Denying him the time to come around completely, Gebu sprang up again and whammed his iron head into his nasal bridge. With a shriek, blood squirted from his broken nose and filled his mouth. Losing his balance, he lurched backward.

Gebu was about to grab his handgun when the short gangster found himself on the right side of the tall gangster.

As soon as this reckless thug showed his face, he fired at Gebu.

It was too late for Gebu to dodge the bullet.

Bang!

It was a close shave! The bullet skimmed over Gebu's back and slit his black shirt.

Gebu broke out in cold sweat.

He turned around nimbly. Having no time to grab the gun, he pushed the tall gangster with the hand he reached for it. The tall gangster fell on his back over his short partner.

Seeing that Gebu let him go, the tall gangster raised his gun and aimed at Gebu's chest…

Bang!

A fire was shot.

But it was not a shot from the tall gangster's gun.

Therefore, the one who was hit was not Gebu.

It turned out that the short gangster was eager to get the upper hand of Gebu. So, he could not help pulling the trigger. The bullet, the second he had targeted at Gebu, now hit his tall accomplice falling his way.

The bullet went straight into the tall gangster's chest and pierced through his heart.

With his mouth wide open, he plunked on his back with a thump.

The short gangster was stupefied.

Gebu leapt to his front and spat a mouthful blood onto his face.

Not knowing what the spit was and only feeling it sticky and metallic, the short gangster presumed that Gebu was casting a spell over him. So, he turned and took to his heels with terror.

Gebu started chasing him as soon as he picked up the tall gangster's gun.

Why did the short gangster flee while holding a gun in his hand?

He was simply scared out of his wits.

A man on the run flees in any direction he stumbles in.

He had just taken a few steps when he tripped on the slimy fish and plumped face down on the pebble riverbed.

His fairly properly positioned front teeth were knocked off.

At the same time, the big black carp, taking advantage of the momentum given by the short gangster's slipping foot, flipped back into the river and swam for its life.

Enduring his pain, the short gangster struggled to rise with the push of his hands.

But he found it impossible to move, as if a big stone slab were weighing on his back.

In fact, what was pressed on his back was Gebu's foot.

Digging the gun into the back of his head, Gebu commanded in a hushed voice,

"Don't move! If you do, I'll blow your brains out!"

"Ow…ow…," moaned the trembling short gangster. "I'm not moving. I'm not…"

"Answer my questions. Who was the guy in the old house? Why did you kill him? Why?"

"I…I…"

The short gangster hemmed and hawed. He pressed his head down trying hard to bury it in the pebbles.

"Will you answer me or not?"

Gebu tapped him on his head with the barrel of his gun.

"I will. I will…"

"Then spit it out!"

"Okay, okay…"

The short gangster kept saying okay…

Then, he suddenly went crazy and began to scream at the top of his lungs:

"Come on quick! Stop the thief!"

Gebu was stunned. Looking up in the distance, he saw three people running his way on the riverbank in the moonlight.

Pressing his ear on the dry riverbed, the short gangster had heard their footsteps before bursting into a hysterical cry for help.

"See if you can scream again!"

Angry as well antsy, Gebu pulled the trigger…

Bang!

The short gangster's head was instantly drenched in blood.

Gebu wiped off the blood that had spattered his face. He looked up and saw the people running his way were drawing nearer and nearer.

It was impossible to run away along the riverbed in such bright moonlight.

Picking up the short gangster's gun and tucking it in his belt, Gebu took a few strides and threw himself into Nanla River...

Chapter 9

The torrential river rushed him downstream instantly.

Slanting himself transversely in the water, Gebu swam toward the other bank.

The current was too rapid for him to set feet on the beach. As a result, he was washed down again for quite some distance.

Eventually, he got hold of a small tree and pulled himself onto the bank with great effort.

Only then did he find one of the handguns already swept away.

The beard attached to his face was also swept away by the torrent.

After shaking the water off his clothes, he hid the remaining gun in a tree hollow. Then, he headed straight for the Loquat Horse Caravan Inn taking long strides.

Luckily, it was still dark, and the guests in the inn were still fast asleep.

Gebu sneaked back to his room, which he found in the same condition as it had been when he left it.

He heaved a sigh of relief.

Escaping from danger is not a victory.

There're too much questions to answer…

First and foremost, I must find out if the victim in the old house was Weng Guo or not.

If it was him, then, the liaison is cut off.

Moreover, who's Green Bamboo Viper?

These thugs who killed a man, moved his body, and have firearms must be connected with Mountain Wind or Iron's Head…

Gebu was wide awake in bed throughout the night.

Day broke. People began to come and go from the inn. Horses neighed. Roosters crowed cock-a-doodle-doo.

Another day of hustle and bustle began.

Gebu changed into laundered shirts and pants, slung the snake sack over his shoulder, and stepped out of his room. He walked up to the row of rooms where Swarthy Guotou was staying.

He caught sight of Boss Lu helping Swarthy Guotou collect the rice grains.

His attention was again drawn to the lengthy row of horseback loads tied with red cloth ribbons.

It is only too natural for horseback loads of almost all horse caravans look the same and therefore be misidentified when put side by side. Such mistakes can be absolutely avoided by the ribbon markings.

Approaching with quickened pace, he greeted them loudly, "Good morning, Boss Lu and Bro Swarthy!"

The two turned around simultaneously.

Only then did Gebu realize that he greeted the right person in Boss Lu. But he misidentified the other one. Instead of being Swarthy Guotou. He merely resembled him in appearance and shape. There was no questioning that he was his brother.

Boss Lu nodded, his smiling round eyes closing to slits so that the wrinkles at their corners looked like unfolded tiny hand fans.

"Had a good sleep last night?"

"Yes, I did, Boss Lu."

Boss Lu unexpectedly shook his head.

"I don't think so. Your eyes are as red as a rooster's comb."

Gebu's heart skipped a beat.

Did he say it without meaning it or allude to something?

"Ha-ha," Gebu chuckled. "It's too embarrassing to say. Last night, I heard mice stirring along the wall outside my room. Thinking that there're snakes where there're mice, I got up and kept an eye on their appearance at the base of the wall. I hoped I could catch one and have it fixed for Boss Lu and Brother Swarthy as a token of my gratitude. Who would expect that there should be no trace of snakes throughout the night?"

Boss Lu broke into a laughter:

"Ha-ha-ha! Of course, you saw no snakes. Knowing a snake catcher is here, what snake dares to come out? I've heard that snake meat tastes better than chicken, but it can't be fixed in the kitchen. They say if the soot fell from the ceiling into the cooking pot, the snake's spirit would haunt people."

Boss Lu had just finished when Swarthy Guotou boomed behind him:

"Boss Lu, while it's been a long time since you harvested your loquat berries, we can still smell their fragrance! You see, I met with this gentleman while I was eating *tangyuan*[9] for my breakfast in the street. He's looking for your inn to stay."

Gebu saw a man dressed in the ethnic Blang costume following Swarthy Guotou into the inn.

Behind him trailed a train of four horses each with a load on its back.

The man was of medium height and had a round, chubby face. His broad-bean-like eyes looked distinctly black and white. The broad-rimmed felt hat on his head betrayed his identify as a small merchant.

---

[9] *"tangyuan"* is a Chinese dish. Traditionally eaten to celebrate the Lantern Festival on the fifteenth day of the first Chinese lunar month, it consists of balled dumplings of glutinous rice flour and various kinds of fillings, mostly boiled and served with soup.

Upon hearing Swarthy Face's introduction, the man hastily folded his hands in salute to Boss Lu.

"My name's Sebo. I'm a salt merchant, yours humbly. I've long heard about Boss Lu's hospitality, kindness, and sincerity towards his guests. So, that's why I've come to your inn. Please excuse me if my stay should bring you any inconvenience."

"Ah, please don't stand on ceremony! As an old saying goes, 'Mountains face mountains; people meet people.' It's fate and good luck that bring us all here from different parts of the country." Beaming, Boss Lu went up to receive the guest. He continued, "Sorry that my rooms are all small with insufficient amenities. Please forgive me should it make you feel uncomfortable."

After he finished, Boss Lu led this salt merchant away to settle him in a room.

Gazing at the four horseback loads, Gebu whispered to Swarthy Guotou:

"He's got quite a lot of salt. Don't know if it's good quality."

"So, you're interested in buying some, aren't you?" Swarthy Guotou responded, "I've checked. Good quality, genuine salt from time-honored wells."

Gebu nodded, saying, "Yes. If my business goes smoothly, I'll buy some and bring it with me. My line of work requires that I climb mountains and go deep into bamboo forests. When I'm hungry, I just make do with a meal of barbecued bamboo rats or rabbits I happen to catch. Their meat may be nutritious, but it tastes like cotton if not spiced with salt."

"You're right. We feel listless if we don't eat salt. We'd better let you go and find your business opportunities out there; the street is swarming with people."

After thanking him, Gebu was about to leave, when Swarthy Guotou stopped him, saying,

"You're a stranger here. Don't run around recklessly. Whether having a deal or not, return to the inn as early as possible. Never wait till dark. I hear say that there were gunshots on the dry riverbed last night."

"Gee," exclaimed Gebu with pretentious surprise, "Really?"

"I heard it from an old man in the *tangyuan* dumpling eatery. I also heard that Weng Guo and his people went to catch the perpetrator early in the morning."

What? Weng Guo?

He's still alive?

Gebu was seized with secret joy. He asked in a haste,

"Did they catch anyone?"

Swarthy Guotou shook his head.

"I heard all this in the *tangyuan* eatery. Not sure if it's true or not."

"Thank you, Bro! I'll be back to our inn whether I have a deal or not."

"One more thing I'd like to tell you. Our grain is air dried. So, we're ready to leave tomorrow morning."

"What? You're leaving tomorrow?"

"Fish in the same river will swim back to meet again. Go ahead to the street first. Come to my room when you return, and we'll have a drink."

Parting with Swarthy Guotou, Gebu stepped out of the inn and onto the street.

The street was already busy. Both its sides teemed with stalls selling diverse vegetables, fishes and meats, fruits and melons, as well as miscellaneous items of daily necessity. Various street cries were deafening as shoppers elbowed and pushed one another in the packed. Focusing on the merchandise rather than on the people, some marketgoers stepped on each other's toes or treaded on the back of each other's shoes. Sweating profusely, small merchants who came late squeezed their way through the crowd leading their horses through rising dust and permeating stench of human perspiration and animal dung. As they plowed ahead, they yelled out excuses for people to make way. Tagging after each of their horses was a group of people taking advantage of the animals' furrowing prowess. As they staggered along, they kept glancing at the merchandise flanking the street.

Gebu also squeezed himself into the crowd.

His destination was the *tangyuan* dumpling eatery.

He wanted to hear from the old man in it what he knew about what had transpired last night.

In addition, he also wanted to know if Weng Guo had led his people in search of the perpetrator.

If everything is true and Weng Guo is still alive, I'll

find him today come what may.

While contemplating, Gebu moved along with the crowd involuntarily.

He could not hold his steps, like it or not.

He was moving along when suddenly someone shouted,

"Mind you, don't get bumped by my horse!"

Gebu dodged hastily, barely slamming his face into that of a pony.

Soon afterwards, he unexpectedly heard another cry:

"Excuse me, my horse's coming!"

Gebu turned around abruptly only to face a horse baring its white teeth, which almost dug into his waist.

As he was getting quickly out of the horse's way, he suddenly spotted, among the bobbing heads of the crowd, a pair of eyes that looked out of the ordinary.

Only Gebu who always had to put his life on the line could detect something ominous in something that looked uneventful.

This pair of extraordinary eyes were being fixed steadily upon Gebu through the crowd.

The grim look helped Gebu instantly single out the pair of eyes behind it from the crowd.

Pretending to dodge the horse, he turned around and stole another glance at the man who were shadowing him.

What he saw startled him…

Of the two spying eyes, one was higher than the other!

No, the dislocation of the eyes was not innate. They were pulled out of place by a knife scar running from the top of his forehead down to between his eyebrows.

Gosh! Scarface!

Is that he?

Why is he shadowing me?

Is he likely to be the thin and lanky man I saw last night?

Did he identify me as the one on the dry riverbed?

If so, I must get rid of him by all means!

How?

The street is narrow and full of people and horses coming and going. I must think of a perfect way of putting him away.

Gebu contemplated while plowing through the crowd.

Now, the *tangyuan* dumpling eatery was already in sight in front of him.

Not far away was a stall where a variety of side swords were spread on the ground for sale.

The sharp edges of the side swords gave him an idea.

Good! When the guy comes near me, I'll strike him with one of the swords and run into the *tangyuan* eatery in the commotion.

Gebu looked up and took a glance at the eatery ahead.

As if thinking of the eatery with customers coming in and out as not busy enough, a magician's troupe was preparing for an outdoor performance by establishing a perimeter with a piece of printed cloth fabric. A plump woman with a decorative paper flower planted in her hair was hawking at the top of her lungs by the perimeter's entrance:

> Come and watch wonderful shows,
>
> Out of a flower vase a head grows.
>
> How can a head grow from a vase?
>
> A ticket will let you see face to face.
>
> Come and watch a rare person,
>
> Come and see an odd woman.
>
> She has no head but only a body,
>
> She's real and as alive as can be.
>
> She's not a ghost but a living human being.
>
> She can eat apart from talking and singing…

Gebu walked up to the stall selling the side swords, bent down, and picked one up.

It was a fantastic sword!

Its cutting edges shone, and its tip was sharp.

Gebu tested the edge's sharpness by running his thumb perpendicularly across it.

He pretended to choose swords to buy, waiting for Scarface to come over.

People squeezed by Gebu to watch the "Beauty in the Vase."

The plumb woman hawked with more enthusiasm:

> You pay to visit Shanghai and Nanjing,
>
> To see something rare and bewitching.

But the thing both odd and rare is here,

You'll sure regret missing what's queer,

Come to our show you to fascinate,

Buy your tickets, don't you hesitate.

Watching a show will make you live longer…

Hearing that it was rare and old and would lengthen lives, more people came to watch.

Gebu looked back only to find Scarface gone.

Gee, where's he?

Where can he be?

Did I scare him away with the sword in my hand?

Gebu stopped searching with his eyes and squeezed into the crowd that was eager to watch the "Beauty in the Vase."

When the people behind him blocked his view, he stepped aside and sneaked into the *tangyuan* eatery, where he found a table and sat down.

Sitting across him was an inconspicuous old man of a small stature. He was eating the *tangyuan* dumplings from a big bowl he was holding with both hands.

There were quite a few customers in the eatery, some sitting down to munch as soon as they paid at the cashier, and others carrying the *tangyuan* out to enjoy them at home.

Gebu directed his eyes at the cashier's counter only to see a plump old woman instead of an old man.

Gebu decided to sit awhile to wait for the old man to return and resume cooking *tangyuan*. He would then go up to accost him under the pretext of purchasing the dumplings.

While waiting, Gebu kept an eye on the entrance, searching the crowd for Scarface's sudden appearance.

After a while, the old man still did not return. Gebu could not help feeling anxious.

Just then, the little old man eating *tangyuan* across him suddenly spoke:

"Hey, why didn't you go and watch the 'Beauty in the Vase'?"

At first, Gebu did not pay any attention, thinking that he was talking to someone else.

But when he took a casual glimpse of him, he found the little old man beaming and slightly inebriated. Squinting his murky and somewhat cunning eyes into the size of mung beans, he was gazing at him.

He seemed as if he were drinking high-proof alcohol instead of eating *tangyuan*.

"Hey, why didn't you go and watch the "Beauty in the Vase?"

The little old man unhurriedly repeated his question.

Now, Gebu heard him loud and clear. He was speaking to him.

"Ah," Gebu nodded slightly and then shook his head, "I don't like it. I don't like to watch it. They're just tricking the audience."

Gebu responded casually and directed his eyes towards the entrance again.

His attention was not focused on the inconspicuous little old man.

But the little old man was very much interested in him.

He looked either really drunk or so bored that he desired to talk with someone.

"It's true they trick people," said the little old man, fixing his mung-bean-like eyes on Gebu's face. He wished that Gebu could look back and exchange an expression with him.

But Gebu did not turn to look at him.

Unaffected by Gebu's indifference, the little old man kept on prattling:

"A vase is a vase after all. How can a head grow out of it? Yep, we don't have to watch it. We'll know it's a trick just by listening to the plump woman's street cry. You're not interested in this tricky magic show, are you?

Reticent Gebu only nodded.

The little old man asked again,

"What do you think is interesting then?"

Gebu felt a bit annoyed.

Why is this little old man so persistent and silly?

Gebu simply stopped heeding him.

But the little old man did not mind Gebu's slight. He said half intoxicatedly, "I bet you'll be intrigued if I write a character."

Upon hearing this, Gebu suddenly realized that the little old man was neither boring nor silly.

He turned around and stared at the little old man.

"What did you say?"

Instead of responding to him, the beaming little old man looked at him fixedly with his turbid, somewhat cunning eyes squinted into the size of mung beans. After a while, he hung his head down. Unhurriedly, he dipped a chopstick into the remaining soup in his bowl and wrote on the table stroke by stroke.

He wrote a character.

It was as big as a fist...

Snake!

Gebu was stunned!

But his did not show it in his expression.

Suppressing his astonishment, he chuckled:

Ha-ha! How do you know I'm interested in snakes?"

The little man gave an irrelevant answer:

"Because I'm also interested in snakes."

Gebu blinked his eyes and said,

"Aha, you said so because you saw my snake sack. So, it means that you're also doing snake business, aren't you?"

The irresponsive little old man kept smiling.

Gebu, too, affected a smile.

In a situation like this, affected smiles are better than any words.

Smirking for a few seconds, the little old man said emphatically word by word:

"No. But I've got snakes to sell you, if you're really in the business."

Gebu raised his voice:

"You think I am tricking you like a magician, don't you?"

The little old man suddenly dropped his smile.

"That's great. I'm keeping my snakes at home, which is pretty faraway. I'll go and get the snakes right away. We'll decide the price when you see what you buy. I'll never over-charge you."

Gebu said, "Deal! When will you return?"

The little old man replied, "Towards the evening."

Gebu asked further, "Where shall I wait for you?"

Reaching his finger, the little old man pointed while asking, "Do you see that big banyan tree in the distance?"

Gebu looked into the distance and was stunned again…

It was at the banyan tree in front of Weng Guo's house that the little old man was pointing.

The little old man said,

"I'm come on a black horse. Wait for me under the ban-yan tree."

After he finished, he put down his bowl, turned towards the entrance, and without saying goodbye, pushed into the crowd.

The appearance of the little old man was out of the blue.

His designation of the banyan tree as the venue of their

rendezvous was too coincidental.

Gebu now was faced with a predicament: he could neither buy nor give up buying *tangyuan* dumplings; he could neither leave nor stay.

Suddenly, he spotted a familiar figure out of the corner of his eye. It was the boy barely bitten by a king cobra.

"Hello…"

Gebu hollered.

He had to stop short of calling the boy because he suddenly remembered that the boy had not told him his name.

He was not able to call him by his name.

Gebu gave up calling and hurried to the entrance.

But the boy had vanished in thin air.

The plump woman with the paper flower decorating her hair was still hawking loudly:

> Don't you think it rare?
>
> Don't you think it odd?
>
> The rarity you've ne'er dreamed of,
>
> The oddity you've ne'er thought of,
>
> They happen to be here for you…

Gebu broke into a wry smile: it's so true. I've never dreamed of so much rarity and oddity happening to me all at once!

Did the boy come to eat tangyuan as well?

Where was he in the eatery while I was talking with the little old man?

Gebu turned around only to see an empty bowl sitting on the table behind him.

Is the empty bowl the boy's?

Was he hiding behind me just now?

He knows me very well. But, instead of greeting me, he was hiding behind me. Why?

Was he eavesdropping my conversation with the little old man?

Then, why did he have to listen to our conversation in secret?

Who asked him to do so?

And who was the little old man that suddenly appeared before me?

How did he know I'm doing snake business?

A series of questions crowded into Grub's mind.

The little old man's murky little green-bean-like eyes were blinking cunningly and vividly in front of Gebu's mind's eye.

Does he really have snakes to sell?

Am I going to meet him in the evening or not?

Chapter 10

Gebu decided to go to the meeting.

As an old saying goes, "You can't catch the cubs without venturing into the tigress's lair."

Only by meeting the little old man could he figure out his real intent.

This was unquestionably a dangerous move.

But to Gebu, taking risks was as common as eating and sleeping.

What's more, Gebu obviously felt that he had been spied on. If he failed to show up, his opponent would suspect his identity. He might just as well go and act naturally as a real snake merchant.

And he had not yet seen Weng Guo, whom he was to contact.

He could take the opportunity of meeting the little old man under the banyan tree to venture into the old house under the pretext of asking for drinking water.

At dusk, Gebu came to the banyan tree with his snake sack tucked in his waist.

It was quiet under the banyan tree.

It was equally silent in the small yard and the old house.

The red-cedar gate with broad-leaved vines crawling all over was closed tight.

Through the cracks of the bamboo-stem wall encircling the courtyard, Gebu found the two-paneled door to the old house also firmly shut.

Gebu was mulling over the options of visiting the old house under the pretense of asking for drinking water or waiting for the little old man to arrive.

Suddenly, a horse was heard clip-clopping in the distance.

A black horse was galloping over to the banyan tree in the dark of the night.

Black horse!

The little old man was coming indeed.

Was he coming with the snakes?

As the clip-clopping drew nearer and nearer, Gebu became increasingly intense.

What if he's a viper himself?

Kill him?

No!

I mustn't kill unless I have no alternatives.

Close by a residential area, this is not the right place for killing.

Besides, he is definitely not the only person who knows our meeting.

If I killed him, I'd disclose my identity.

Even though they've been shadowing me, they've no reason to suspect my identity.

Once I kill one of them, I'll tell them who I am.

Then, how can I accomplish my mission?

No, I can't do it. I must keep calm.

As he was contemplating, the black horse had reached him.

He looked up, only to be shocked…

There was no one on its back.

What?

Before Gebu collected himself, the horse was startled by the sight of a figure standing in the shadow of the banyan tree. It neighed and reared up.

Gebu dodged the horse in time. Meanwhile, he heard a thump! With it, something fell from its back.

The thing sounded very heavy.

When it came down on its forelegs, the black horse galloped away barely brushing Gebu.

Looking closely, Gebu found on the ground was a gunny sack tied firmly.

In the cube-shaped sack there was a wooden box.

Are these the snakes that the little old man delivered?

But where is he?

Why just the goods without the owner?

Didn't we agreed upon discussing the price when we see the snakes?

Perplexed, Gebu went up and gave the gunny sack a

kick, but what his toes felt was not a wooden box.

Producing a small, snake-cutting knife from his waist, he sliced the gunny sack. As soon as he peeped into the opening, he broke into cold sweat all over…

A bloody human head was staring at him with wide-open eyes.

Beneath the head was the body dissected into several pieces.

"Yikes!" Gebu could not help screaming!

The blood-covered head had a black, bushy beard…

What? Big Beard!

Weng Guo!

Gebu's hands trembled.

Weng Guo was murdered.

The bloody body he laid his hand on when fumbling in the old house was Weng Guo's!

The news that Weng Guo went to catch someone in the morning was fake.

"Just go to him. His bark is worse than his bite, so to speak. You won't be disappointed. In my opinion, he must have scared all the girls away with his barks and remains a single, as single as a tree."

Swarthy Guotou's words rang again in Gebu's ears.

His bark is worse than his bite. He is as single as a tree.

But today, the tree is cut down…

The arrowhead carved on the half of the kemu tally he had sent out would never be able to match the shaft and fletching carved on the other half.

With Weng Guo's death and Kaluo's temporary absence in Caoluo Street, Gebu found that he had no one to consult.

The next move was laden with more difficulty and danger.

The opponent Green Bamboo Viper is indeed a cunning and ruthless viper!

But when does a red-faced mongoose falter in front of a venomous snake?

As long as I see one, I must charge over. This is what a red-faced mongoose does as its nature dictates.

With this thought, Gebu sprang up to his feet…

Since the little old man set a trap here, there must be ambush nearby.

Just then, the red-cedar gate opened with a squeak. Soon, two burly men armed with handguns leapt out.

"Hey, murderer, we've been waiting here for ages!"

Gebu gave a start of astonishment and realized the vicious intent of the thugs.

They wanted to frame him.

The burly men rushed over leveling their handguns. Gebu knew that if he should engage in a fight with them, he would not have been able to claim to be a snake merchant anymore.

He yelled, "I'm here to buy snakes! I'm not a killer!"

After yelling, he took flight.

"Run after him!"

"Don't let him get away! He killed our deputy leader Weng Guo!"

The two burly men scrambled to their feet and ran after Gebu, who had covered half a kilometer by now.

Gebu had two nimble legs like wings. He could run as fast as lightning.

He had displayed his supernatural speed and stamina in many an act of pursuit or retreat.

He was no exception this time.

Whoosh, whoosh, and whoosh!

Whoosh, whoosh, and whoosh!

He heard only the wind rushing by.

Fast, fast, and fast!

Fast, fast, and fast!

He ran as fast as his legs could carry him.

Gebu had left the two men far behind.

In his black clothing, he appeared like an arrow darting forward in the dark of the night.

The two burley men were hot in pursuit, running while shouting:

"Stop! If you don't, we'll shoot!"

To dodge the expected bullets, Gebu did not run in a straight line. Instead, he adopted the "snaking" tactic he had learned while catching snakes.

Changing directions all the time, he ran like a winding snake.

The pursuers could not aim at their target at all.

Surprisingly, the two men only threatened to open fire but never pulled their triggers.

If they fired randomly together, it would be impossible for Gebu to escape a bullet or two.

Their bark is worse than their bite. Why so?

Gradually, Gebu ran into the residential area full of courtyards of houses.

Increasing obstacles on his way slowed him down.

Just then, the two men hot in pursuit raised their voice intentionally:

"Stop thief!"

"Catch the killer!"

"He killed our deputy leader Weng Guo!"

The two thugs' brazenness indicates they're known as militiamen.[10]

When militiamen cry "Catch the thief," some of the residents will definitely come out to help them.

If they should stop me without knowing what's really going on, I'd be in grave danger.

"Stop him!"

---

[10] Militiamen are the civilian part of the Police-Civilian Integrated Defense Team (PCIDT)

"Catch him!"

The pursuers were closing the distance.

Gebu could not run further. He had to find a place to hide.

He turned into an alley in the residential area. There was a courtyard with adobe walls within his reach.

He looked up and found the wall a little above his height. He could just spring up onto it and leap into the courtyard hands down.

Once in a courtyard, he could surely find a hiding place.

He tiptoed to the door to the courtyard and was about to peep into it through the crack of the door when suddenly he heard a creak. Not far behind him, the door to another courtyard opened.

Gebu was taken aback. He was about to turn and flee when someone rushed out of the door and grabbed him by the arm.

Gebu looked back only to find none other than the anonymous boy he had rescued.

The boy fixed his big eyes on Gebu.

There was not a hint of startle in his eyes as if he was prepared for anything that could come to pass.

Thumping footsteps were heard coming from a near distance.

The thugs were catching up with him.

The boy gave Gebu's arm a tug.

"Go in!"

He said only two words.

But he said them quietly and forcefully, with a tone of indisputable coercion.

Thump, thump, thump!

The pursuing footfalls were coming even nearer.

Without time to hesitate, Gebu leapt into the courtyard.

The door was immediately shut quietly behind him.

When Gebu looked back, however, he found that the boy had not followed him into the courtyard.

The yard was relatively small, with two small, low bungalows on its two sides.

The doors in the houses were closed. Against the east wall, a big bundle of boughs and branches were leaning, apparently fireworks for cooking.

Gazing at the bundle of branches, Gebu pondered that entering the houses without knowing what was in them would put him in a disadvantageous position. He might as well hide in the bundle first.

He had just huddled in the bundle when he heard the two burly men yelling outside the yard:

"Argh, he vanished after flashing in front of us. How come?"

"There's no way he'll ever escape us! He must be hiding in one of the residences!"

"Let's search each of them!"

The shouts soon approached the door to this courtyard.

Just then, footfalls of running were heard outside the door.

The two thugs heard the footfalls and cried with astonishment, "Hey, he's running away!"

The footfalls quickly led them away from the door.

Gebu knew that it was the boy that was doing so.

He took a deep breath and immediately felt worried: what if the thugs took hold of the boy?

Sure enough, he heard the thugs roaring in the distance, "It's you, rascal! What are you running for? Eh?"

"I'm helping you catch the thief! He's just passed by!"

The two thugs fell silent.

The boy was also heard saying, "Are you running after a man with a cloth sack with him?"

The thugs shouted:

"Yes, yes! He's a murderer!"

"He ran in the west. He's fast runner."

"Let's run after him!"

"Yes, let's run after him!"

Thump, thump, and thump!

The thugs ran in the west.

Taking a deep breath and wiping off the sweat from his face, Gebu rose and went out of the bundle of branches.

I can't stay here for long.

If the thugs run in the west for a while and can't find me, they are most likely to return.

Gebu was about to get out of the courtyard when the bundle of boughs and branches behind him was pushed cracking down, revealing a huge hole in the adobe wall of the house.

It turned out that the hole was shielded by the bundle, and when he had sneaked into it, he had directed his eyes on the door and trained his ears on the movements outside the courtyard only. He was not aware of the fairly large hole behind him.

Hearing the bundle falling, he was about to turn around when someone darted out of the hole and pounced on him from behind. Before Gebu had time to dodge the attack, a coir rope flew whooshing around his neck.

The tragic incident of him being almost strangled in a coir rope lasso was about to repeat itself.

The tactic was so familiar.

Gebu reached to grab the coir rope…

But it was not tightened at once.

A chilly voice assailed his eardrums from behind like a piercing needle:

"Don't move! Follow me if you want me to spare your life!"

The voice was so familiar!

Gebu turned around only to see a scarred face…

The horrific Scarface!

Chapter 11

With the end of the coir rope in his hand, Scarface crawled out of the hole and led Gebu into another courtyard.

This courtyard was even smaller and had a dilapidated small adobe house in it.

The small house appeared nearly burned down. Without windows or doors, the dark, framed opening where windows used to be installed were covered with spider webs. The cracks in the stone staircase in front of the door were overgrown with weeds as tall as a man's height. A broken pottery jar laid by its side with its mouth wide open.

The ruination in the courtyard suggested that it had long been uninhabited.

Scarface dragged Gebu into the small adobe house.

Fire had incinerated everything in the house except the lower part of the four columns, standing charred like four monsters.

Scarface held his steps and, staring at Gebu, said dismally, "We've met before!"

Gebu forced a smile,

"I called you Zhuang Laohan, thinking that you were Zhuang Laoyao's younger brother."

"Are you still looking for Zhuang Laohan?"

"So, you're going to help, aren't you?"

Scarface snorted.

"I've heard you're a snake merchant. You've been to many places and seen the world."

"Yes, because all the snakes at home are wiped out."

Scarface pointed at the small adobe house with his chin.

"Now you tell me. What do you think of this place?"

"It's a good place! After you strangle me to death, no one can find me even when my body was laden with maggots."

"Glad you're aware of it! Don't think you're in a safe when you stay in the Loquat Horse Caravan Inn!" said Scarface. His expression turned ferocious, and with a "whoosh," he pulled his Burmese saber out.

Before Gebu dodged it in time, he had placed the saber horizontally against his throat.

"Tell me! What on earth are you doing?"

The edge of the saber against the skin felt extremely chilly.

Gebu leered at the saber and then at the coir rope.

"If I were a salt merchant, I would have peed in my pants out of fear. I've been dealing with snakes my whole life and coming face to face with death many times. Sabers and ropes are the same as snakes."

The uneven brows on his scarred face twitched vigorously.

"If you're not afraid of death, why did you run?"

"If I die, I must know the cause. I was waiting for the little old man to deliver his snakes to me, and they accused me of killing someone."

"They didn't wrong you at all. You look to me like a murderer. Go and stand against that column." As he demanded, Scarface force Gebu back up to the column and tied him to it.

"You mean now that you're my captive, and you want me to tell you why I'm going to kill you, right?"

"Birds don't swim and dive in water; fish don't flip and flap on mountains. Without knowing the reason of my death, my soul can't ascend to paradise."

Scarface nodded.

"Answer me. What were you up to when you went to the old house under the banyan tree last evening?

Gebu pretended to be shocked:

"What? The old house under the tree? I just told you why I was there, didn't I? I went to see Zhuang Laohan, younger brother of my friend Zhuang Laoyao. I thought he lived in that old house but went to the wrong one, where I ran into you!"

Scarface did not seem angry with Gebu at his pretended naivete.

"That happened in the early evening. What I asked was about the midnight!"

"I didn't go to the old house at midnight."

"Then where did you go?"

"I was dreaming of going to all the beautiful places on my bed."

"What about the dry riverbed?"

Gebu's heart jumped a beat. He realized how cunning Scarface was!

"Ha-ha-ha!" Gebu laughed, "That's the only place I didn't go. I heard that gunshots were fired last night on the riverbed. They even asked me why I didn't go and enjoy the excitement."

"If you didn't go to the riverbed, you were not in bed, either!"

"What? So, you went to see me in the horse caravan inn? Do you mean you know Laohan's whereabouts already?"

"Don't give me the nonsense about Laohan. Tell me why you didn't sleep in bed last night!"

Gebu shrugged.

"Didn't you see me crouching at the base of the wall?"

Scarface apparently did not catch what he said.

Gebu began to explain in every detail:

"I meant I was wondering if you saw me squatting along the wall outside my hotel room. To be frank with you. I was lying on my bed last night when I heard mice squeaking outside my room. Believing the presence of mice to be an indicator of snakes, I wanted to catch one for the owner of the inn so he could enjoy it as a delicacy. Who would expect that I didn't even see a scale of a snake with all the time I spent the whole night? And, in the end, I also missed your visit. I had asked you to help me locate Laohan earlier in the evening, and you came to tell me about his whereabouts late at night. Please tell me now where he is, won't you?"

"Argh! You never stop talking about Laohan, making believe that he really exists."

Pointing the tip of the blade against Gebu's throat, Scarface lowered his voice:

"Tell me the truth. You're here at Caoluo Street to see Weng Guo, aren't you?"

Hushed as it was, the voice sounded like a needle piercing into his lungs.

Fixing his eyes on the saber, Gebu suddenly raised his voice:

"Do it quick if you want to kill me. Who's Weng Guo? I don't know him. I'm a snake merchant. I'm here at Caoluo Street just to scrape a living."

Scarface sized Gebu up and down with his chilling eyes.

Suddenly, he reached out and pulled Gebu's headwear open.

Clack!

The bamboo kemu tally hidden in the headwear dropped to the ground.

It happened that the tally landed face up, clearly showing the carved arrowhead.

Gebu had never expected that Scarface would have such a trick in his sleeve.

Pointing at the tally, Scarface questioned:

"Scraping a living with this?"

Gebu remained silent.

Scarface questioned closely, "What's it for?"

Gebu laughed a bitter laugh, "You may laugh at me if I tell you. It's my talisman!"

"Talisman?"

"Yes, it has only the staff of an arrow. Without an arrowhead, it can kill people. Traveling with the talisman, it can protect me from any spear thrust in the open and any arrow shot in secret."

Frowning, Scarface blurted out: "Nonsense!"

Gebu said chuckling, "Okay, even though I'm talking nonsense, take a look at what this is!"

Scarface was dumbfounded.

Just then, a rock as big as a man's fist flew whishing from outside the courtyard and fell thumping to the ground.

Scarface gave a shudder and soon collected himself. He stuffed Gebu's headcloth into his mouth. Then, he walked around the column to make sure he was tied securely with the coir rope. Then, he glared at Gebu, saying:

"Though a merchant, you can make lies sound truer than facts. You think I don't know what you're up to, don't you?"

As soon as he finished, he stepped out of the small room and sneaked to the door along the wall.

He pressed his ear on the door and listened for a while before he pushed it open abruptly and leaped out.

What Gebu heard next was a clunk. The door was locked from outside.

Silence reigned in the dilapidated courtyard.

Gebu squirmed a bit but found the coir rope extremely tight.

He could neither run away nor cry out.

Looking down, his eyes fell on the kemu tally on the ground.

Strange! How did Scarface know I hid the kemu in my headcloth?

While I was hiding my handgun prior to entering Caoluo Street, I concealed the *kemu* in my headcloth. But how did he know it?

Gebu was racking his brain trying to find an answer when, all of a sudden, a figure flashed at the back window.

Wow! A figure as nimble as a sparrow leaped into the room from the rear window.

It was none other than the boy!

With a knife held between his teeth, he darted over and quickly cut off the coir rope. He then yanked the headcloth out of Gebu's mouth.

"You…"

With his hands free, Gebu was about to say something when the boy placed his hands over his mouth. He then tucked the knife on his waist and threw his head towards the window.

Gebu sprang up like a leaping tiger or a soaring dragon and vaulted through the rear window.

He landed quietly and looked around, and he found a large breach beneath the rear window caused by the partially collapsed wall.

Without hesitation, Gebu stotted out of the wall like a gazelle jumping over a stream.

Before he balanced himself, he heard a thump behind.

Gebu turned around and found the boy to have just landed steadily.

Gebu cried out, "Good boy, why, why are you saving me?"

The boy threw his head up and said, "Didn't you save me once? Why did you do it then?"

Gebu smiled, "Because a venomous snake was trying to bite you."

While saying so, he put his hand around the boy's shoulder and continued, "Thank you, child!"

Unexpectedly, the boy responded, "When you saved me, I didn't say 'thank-you'."

"Do you know Scarface, child?"

The boy did not answer him directly:

"Why did he tie you up? Why did the two people run after you?"

Gebu replied shrugging, "Well, I want to know why myself."

"Do you?" asked the boy blinking his big eyes.

"Suddenly, he reached his hand to Gebu and said, "Maybe this is the reason why, isn't it?"

Gebu looked down at his hand and gave a secret shudder.

Held in the boy's hand was the kemu tally that had dropped to the ground.

Before Gebu reached o take it, the boy had already put it in his hand. Meanwhile, he gazed at Gebu with a strange look.

After a moment, he blurted out, "Uncle, the person you're looking for has been murdered."

Gebu's heart skipped a beat.

The boy's words were beyond his expectation.

But it was exactly what he had expected.

Gebu gazed into the boy's eyes.

In them, he saw honesty, sympathy, and a kind of anxiety normally unseen in a child's eyes.

In fact, Gebu had long been fond of him.

For now, the boy might not be quite aware of his fondness.

But deep in his heart, Gebu had already treated him as a friend.

But now, how could he answer the questions put forward by the boy who had saved him twice?

Feelings can soften the heart indeed.

Gebu had never been perturbed by mixed feelings like today.

He really did not want to lie to the boy.

But he responded instead:

"What hocus-pocus are you talking here, child? I've come to Caoluo Street to do my snake business."

The boy daggered him with his eyes.

Saying nothing, he darted into the grove nearby and scampered away without looking back.

Watching the boy vanishing into the grove with the blink of an eye, Gebu was seized by indescribable emotions: he felt weighed down as heavily as lead; he also felt uplifted with warmth and hope at the same time.

Behind the boy, there must be an informed adult, a comrade that can be trusted and relied on.

If I can find him and get his help, I can certainly defeat Green Bamboo Viper and accomplish my mission.

But who's the adult? Where's he? How can I find him?

I can only find him through this vigilant boy.

Thinking of this, Gebu planned to look for the boy. He was about to leave when suddenly he heard something astir behind him. But when he looked back, he saw nothing.

Silence hung in the courtyard.

It prevailed outside the courtyard as well.

Gebu turned around and walked up unhurriedly.

He had taken only two steps when he stopped to look toward the breach in the wall of the courtyard.

From it, a face was half revealed.

Although he caught sight of only half of the face, he saw the knife scar on the forehead clearly.

Yikes, it was Scarface!

Gebu turned and ran away.

Chapter 12

Gebu did not ran in the direction where the boy disappeared for fear that Scarface might discover the trace of the boy.

After running for quite a distance, he realized that no one was pursuing him.

It's strange! Why isn't Scarface chasing me?

Gebu came to a stop. Seeing it getting dark, he decided to return to the Loquat Horse Caravan Inn.

Instead of following a straight route, he took a few roundabout trips. Only then did he head toward the inn after making sure that there was no one following him.

It was pitch dark when he returned to the inn.

When he passed by the row of houses where Back Guotou stayed, he found no lights in his room.

The horseback loads tied with red cloth ribbons were orderly placed under the eaves.

As they would set out early tomorrow morning, they had already gone to sleep.

Gebu thought of rising earlier tomorrow morning to help them with harnessing the horses or placing the loads onto their backs.

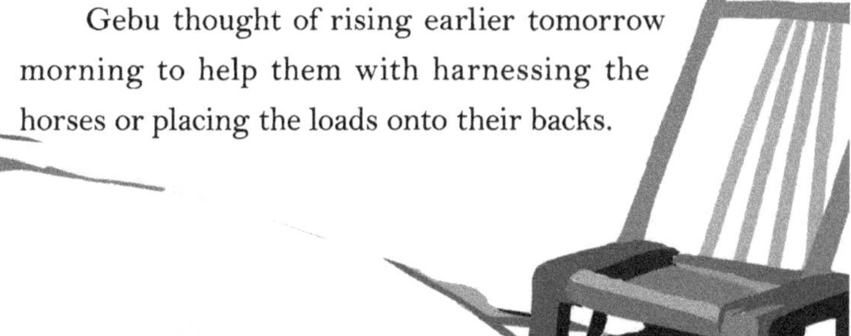

While contemplating, he sneaked into the backyard and reached his own room.

He did not enter immediately.

He stopped to listen by pressing his ear on the door.

It was completely quiet inside.

He turned to look at the rest of the horse caravan inn in the dark.

It was also silent.

Occasionally, there came a couple of snorts from the horses.

"Don't think you're in a safe when you stay in the Loquat Horse Caravan Inn!"

The Scarface's dismal voice suddenly rang in Gebu's ears.

What did he mean by saying that?

A threat?

Or a reminder?

It must be threat.

To Gebu, Scarface posed a threat indeed.

He knew too much.

Moreover, what he wanted to know further was what Gebu tried to protect at all cost.

Therefore, he would never let Gebu off easily.

Gebu was wondering if, by refraining from chasing him now, Scarface would come to capture him in his room since he already knew where he was staying.

It's very probable.

I mustn't go to sleep tonight.

Neither must I lie in bed.

Okay, I'll lie beneath the bed and leave the rear window open so that I'll have a route of retreat.

Having made up his mind, Gebu pulled the door open.

He had just opened the door when a man with his faced masked rushed out of the room.

The man wielded a wooden cudgel in his hand and aimed it at Gebu's head.

How could Gebu dodge such a strike that came as fast as whirlwind and lightning?

Wham!

The cudgel hit ferociously on Gebu's head.

Gebu did not even make an utterance. Holding his head with his hands, he backed a few steps and dropped thumping to the ground.

After writhing a little, he stopped moving.

Blood oozed through his fingers and covered his face.

Thinking that he had overwhelmed Gebu, Horse Face cast away the cudgel and reached both his hands to strangle Gebu.

But before he could get in contact with Gebu, two spears sprang up whooshing from the ground.

A pair of sharp spearheads dug into Horse Face's pit of stomach.

Pouncing upon Gebu on the ground with all the force he had summoned, Horse Face had not been able to anticipate this sudden thrust of the spears from below. The kinetic energy from both directions was almost fatal.

"Ouch…"

Giving a muffled moaning, he fell back holding his stomach.

The two spears rising from the ground were but Gebu's "iron" feet!

Horse Face's sudden strike had only broken the skin on Gebu's head. However, Gebu had pretended to receive a fatal blow with a view of buying time. He had fallen on his back with twofold purposes: to dodge a second strike and to lure his opponent to pounce upon him like a starved tiger so that he could take advantage of the doubled velocity to give the opponent a hard kick at his chest with increased kinetic energy.

It was a brutal kick!

And it was a bullseye!

While Horse Face fell holding his pit of stomach, Gebu withdrew his feet and, using the momentum, sprang up like a flipping fish. He then planted himself on the ground as upright as a pagoda.

Gebu immediately saw another man dashing out. With buzz-cut hair, he also masked his face with a black cloth as well.

From their burly stature, Gebu already recognized them as the two "militiamen" who had chased him a moment before.

Horse Face falling under the impact of Gebu's kick was bumped into by the charging man with his buzz cut hair.

A bloody fight was imminent.

There was no way of evading it.

As the two thugs were both masked, Gebu did not have to treat them as militiamen as they pretended. He could use a strategy of beating them at their own game and teach them a good lesson.

If they're injured, they'll be lucky to have their unworthy lives spared.

If they're killed, they'll be fit for attending to the King of Hell when he pees.

While thinking, Gebu was bursting with uncontrollable strength, balling his hands crackling into fists.

He blurted out:

"Stop the thieves!"

He did unto them what they had done to him during their pursuit of him.

Immediately after his cry for stopping thief, he lunged forward relentlessly. Aiming the tip of his foot at Horse Face's temple, he launched a front snack kick.

As powerful as a thousand-pound hammer, such a kick would smash his sphenoid bone.

Probably Horse Face was destined not to die. The time the kick was flying in the air, Buzz Cut darted out and bumped into his back, causing him to slant his body. Missing his temple, the kick slammed into his jaw and dislocated his features. With the impact, Horse Face flopped to the ground as if his spine had been pulled away from him.

His eyes redden with wrath, Buzz Cut bolted over Horse Face and, gathering up a great deal of strength to his right fist as big as a ham, threw a punch whooshing at Gebu's chest—a move known as "a leopard gouging out his enemy's heart."

Gebu dodged it quickly but felt his shoulder hit and numbed.

Seeing his strike amiss, Buzz Cut lunged a step forward and launched another punch at Gebu's face.

This tactic of one lightning punch after another proved too much for Gebu. With a loud wham, it hit him between the brows.

This strike was so ferocious that Gebu felt his eyes almost pop, and his nose started bleeding. He could hardly keep himself balanced while his head swam.

He knew that if he fell, he would lose the whole game.

Thinking that he had gotten the upper hand, Buzz Cut pulled his hands back, balled them, and sent the two fists out, each aimed at one of Gebu's ears.

This was a move called "double ear strike!"

A sudden increase of the pressure would puncture his ear drums and knock him out of consciousness. This is why the strike is so lethal.

It would be impossible for Gebu to sustain such a deathly blow in a condition where his head was already swimming and his nose bleeding.

With the launch of his "double ear strike," Buzz Cut felt he had clinched the victory.

Buzz Cut did not expect that Gebu had thrusted his two palms out between Buzz Cut's reaching arms.

The "double ear strike" opened Buzz Head's chest to Gebu and thereby gave him the opportunity to strike him in the chest with his palms while the former's arms were still in the air.

Thwack!

It sounded as if the palms pounding the wall of a crag.

At the same time, Gebu had reached out a leg and pressed his foot hard on that of Buzz Cut.

With his upper body bent back by the impact of Gebu's palm strike and his foot pinned to the ground by Gebu's, Buzz Cut went down backward like a panel of a wooden door.

As soon as Gebu let his foot go, Buzz Cut thumped to the ground on his back!

Gebu was about to bring his other foot forward to launch a fatal kick at Buzz Cut's stomach when he felt a chill blasting behind him. He knew that Horse Face had picked himself up and was now coming to Buzz Cut's rescue. Gebu immediately turned right on his left foot as an axis and pulled his right foot up in secret.

Gebu turned around only to face Horse Face eye to eye.

"Receive my palm!"

With a loud cry, Gebu plunged his right palm at Horse

Face's nasal bridge in an axing move.

Charging over, Horse Face only focused his attention on fending off the palm strike. He failed to anticipate Gebu's in his crotch with his right foot. Gebu had lifted it in stealth while turning sideways.

This move is "a back thrust of a spear!"

Gebu's battle cry and the demonstration of his palm were but a swashbuckling posture. It was used to cover this crotch-attacking kick.

This kick was right on target.

Horse Face screamed with agony while reaching his hands to cover his crotch.

Gebu lunged forward and gave him a knife hand strike on the back of his neck with his hand, sending him crumbling down and curling into a ball.

Gebu then balled his palms into fists and prepared to pummel his jaws hard.

He would kill Horse Face as a robber!

Bang! A piece of rock suddenly flew over and hit Gebu on his head.

His head swam before he dropped to the ground.

During his fall, he heard Buzz Cut saying,

"We wouldn't've let him get the upper hand of us if we hadn't had the order to catch him alive."

Horse Face urged, "You'd better shut your mouth! Let's carry him away quickly!"

They picked Gebu up.

Gebu lost consciousness before long...

"Brother Gebu! Brother Gebu!"

When Gebu was awoken by people calling him one after another and opened his eyes, he saw a familiar swarthy face smiling at him in the light of a kerosene hurricane lamp.

Ah, it was Swarthy Guotou!

Gebu sat up slightly, only to find himself in Swarthy Guotou's arms.

Boss Lu, the plump inn assistant Langzhe, as well as Swarthy Guotou's brother and others, were all around him with a look of concern.

They were joyous to see him come to.

Swarthy Guotou said, "Brother Gebu, when we heard you cry 'Stop the thieves,' we all rushed over. But unfortunately, we were a bit too late, and the two thugs slipped away through our fingers."

Rubbing Gebu's wounded forehead gently, Boss Lu shook his head apologetically.

"I'm terribly sorry for the trauma you went through! We've never had incidents like this before here in our small inn."

Swarthy Guotou echoed, "Yes, incidents of robbery have happened in other lodgings, but never here in the Loquat Horse Caravan Inn. Luckily, your injury is only skin deep. The bones are intact."

Others nodded in agreement.

It takes a hundred days to heal an injury to the tendons and bones. Then, it would really make people anxious."

"As an old saying goes, 'Everything's fine if you stay home every day, but everything's difficult if you're away from it.'"

While listening to their comments, Gebu still saw the two masked men in his mind's eye.

Sitting up from Swarthy Guotou's arms, he folded his hands as a gesture of gratitude.

"'A muntjac that fell from a cliff was received by a tree; my life was saved by all of you."

The plump inn assistant Langzhe said, "You'd better go to your room and check if anything is missing."

Gebu said grinning, "I've nothing in the room. Except for a snake sack, I'm poor and bare to the bones. These two robbers came faster than I can make my money."

The crowd burst into a guffaw.

Boss Lu said to everyone around Gebu:

"It's pretty late. Please go back to sleep. Thank you all very much. I'll treat you guys to a drinking party for sure."

The crowd dispersed gradually.

Turning to Gebu, Boss Lu said, "This small room was unlucky. Let me give you another one!"

Gebu said waving his hand, "No, you don't have to!"

Swarthy Guotou continued the thread of the discourse, saying, "Well, Bro, how can't you stay away from a room that bodes ill fortune. It may harm your business. You may come and stay with me."

Before Gebu replied, Boss Lu cut in, "Your room is only big enough to accommodate you and your brother. Besides, you need to get up early tomorrow morning. We'd better not squeeze too many people in your room. I've enough unoccupied rooms."

Just then, a voice intervened unhurriedly:

"Bro, please come and stay with me. I've an extra bed in my room. I've just come as a stranger here and would appreciate company."

Gebu looked around and his eyes fell upon the speaker, who was none other than the salt merchant Ni Sebo who had arrived here in the morning.

Boss Lu nodded, "That's great! A muntjac and a red deer are good companions. You can talk about your business together. What do you think, Gebu?"

Boss Lu gazed fixedly at Gebu.

Without a better option, Gebu had to nod his consent.

"A guest must do as his host thinks fit. Boss Lu, thank you very much! Since Brother Ni Sebo is so hospitable, I'd love to make friends with him and enjoy his company."

Then, he turned to Swarthy Guotou:

"Bro, you're setting out tomorrow morning. So, go to bed early. Tomorrow morning, I'll help you with loading the horses. Shipping grain to the prefectural capital, you have to go by the foot of Mount Nanla. Be vigilant against robbers when you travel!"

Swarthy Guotou said, "I was told by the Police-Civilian Integrated Defense Team (PCIDT) this afternoon that they'll dispatch two of their members to escort us. So, don't worry!"

Swarthy Guotou and his brother excuse themselves and left.

Ni Sebo walked ahead, with a kerosene lamp in his hand to illuminate the way. Boss Lu and the inn assistant Langzhe followed, leading the way for Gebu.

As they walked, Gebu visualized the two masked thugs in his mind's eye again.

They escaped?

It was too easy on them!

While thinking so, he was being led by the lamp light through a loquat grove and to the room where Ni Sebo was staying.

This was a standalone house, not connected to any other guestrooms.

Entering it, he saw it extremely clean and tidy.

The rear window was wide-open so that the air in the room was fresh. In the middle, there were two bamboo beds with a square table separating them. The table was flanked by a bamboo stool on either side.

Ni Sebo took off his felt hat. As he smiled, he half-closed his distinctly black-and-white, broad-bean-like eyes into slits:

"Bro, what do you think of this room? Are you okay with it?"

Gebu said beaming, "I'm afraid I'll make your room sordid with the snakes I'll catch."

Ni Sebo said, "Not a problem! Not a problem! We're like the meteors in the sky and grasshoppers on the earth. We must be predestined to get together here."

Boss Lu chimed in, "While you're from different ethnic backgrounds, one from Aini and the other Blang, you're traveling frequently after all. That's why you can be friends at first sight."

As he said so, he waved to Langzhe,

"Langzhe, get wine. It'll help our guests steady their nerves."

Langzhe said "Yes, sir" and left.

Gebu said, "Boss Lu, it's very kind of you! But how about drinking tomorrow?"

Boss Lu said, "How can I feel comfortable? The first time you come to support our business and you've gotten mugged. What else can I do to express my apology? Some free wine is but a small token!"

Gebu said, "Great, Boss Lu! Then let's drink together!"

Ne Sebo echoed, "Yes, let's drink together. I'll contribute some of the jerked muntjac meat I have with me."

Folding his hands in front of him, Boss Lu said, "That a good idea! That's a great idea! But I have to look at my accounts tonight. After drinking, I may become so muddle-headed that I may count one as ten. I must excuse myself from drinking together with you this time. Please go to sleep early after you finish drinking."

Boss Lu said good-night and left.

After seeing Boss Lu off, Gebu and Ni Sebo entered the room and sat across the bamboo table.

Hanging the kerosene hurricane lamp on a bamboo pole, Ni Sebo took a package out of a muntjac-skin travel bag. He opened the banana leaves wrapping the package and revealed the jerked muntjac meat.

It was oily brown and tantalizingly aromatic.

Only then did Gebu feel hungry, so much so that he felt his belly meeting his backbone.

Right at the moment, Langzhe came carrying a calabash gourd decanter of rice wine in one hand and two cups made of bamboo tubes in the other. He pushed open the door with a smile on his face.

"Here comes the 'nerve-readying' wine! It's brewed from the corn harvested this year. It's very good. Only Boss Lu's bosom friends have the privilege of enjoying a wine of such unique bouquet."

While chatting with the guests, Langzhe poured the wine gurgling from the gourd decanter into the bamboo-tube cups.

It was really good wine with its mellowed aroma.

The muntjac jerky was also delectable. They could not wait as they could hear their stomachs rumbling.

After serving the wine, Langzhe said politely, "Enjoy yourselves and please excuse me."

Seeing Langzhe about to leave, Gebu grabbed him by his arm. Holding up one bamboo cup to his mouth, he urged,

"Come on, Come on! Let's drink together! Drink together!"

Langzhe looked embarrassed, saying, "It's a treat from the boss to his guests. I'm an inn assistant only, how can I…"

"Well," Gebu said half-jokingly, "According to our Aini's customs, it's impolite not to entertain a guest with wine. Now that we have it available, isn't it impolite for you not to drink it?"

Just then, Ni Sebo joined Gebu in urging him, "It's true. It's even more impolite not to drink when wine is served. Langzhe, just have this cup before you leave."

Forcing a smile, Langzhe took the bamboo cup.

"Thank both of you very much, then!"

With that, he held the cup to his lips, jerked his head back, and drained the whole cup gurgling in one gulp.

Seeing Langzhe tossing off the cup, Gebu exclaimed, "You're an awesome drinker! Come on, refill the cup and cheers!"

Grinning, Langzhe declined in a raised voice, "Who needs to steady his nerves, me or you? I've got to get up during the night to feed the horses with extra fodder. If I drank too much, I might get drowned in the trough!"

Ni Sebo intervened, "Okay, okay, let him go. Bro, come on, let us enjoy ourselves."

Gebu let go Langzhe.

Folding his hands in front of him, Langzhe said, "Please excuse me. The boss asked me to tell you to go to bed early after drinking."

After Langzhe stepped out, only Gebu and Ni Bose were left in the room.

"Come on, let's drink!"

Ni Sebo urged as he picked up the gourd decanter. He poured some wine into their cups held his up.

"Come, let's drink!"

Then, he opened his mouth wide, emptied the whole cup into it, and gurgled it down.

He flashed the empty cup before Gebu and said, "It's empty now, Bro!"

Gebu also held his cup and said,

"Cheers!"

With that, he held the bamboo cup to his mouth.

After seeing Langzhe and Ni Sebo drink the wine, Gebu's suspicion of anything wrong with it was dispelled.

He was about to drink it when all of a sudden…

Flop!

Something lengthy flew into the rear window.

And it started wriggling as soon as it landed on the floor.

Yikes, a snake!

A black king cobra!

As soon as it touched down, the cobra raised its front quarters and shot a ferocious look from its bulged black eyes. It then stared at Gebu fixedly. Soon, it expanded its neck as wide as the width of a shoulder pole and, hissing loudly, lunged toward Gebu.

What was happening scared Ni Sebo out of his wits. He screamed trembling all over,

"Snake, snake…"

As he screamed, he huddled on the bed.

He was not a snake handler after all.

Gebu was. Putting his bamboo cup down calmly, he said, "Don't be afraid!"

He then pounced on the king cobra.

Seeing Gebu charging at it, the king cobra was even furious.

It darted toward Gebu like a streak of dark lightning, aiming at his leg.

Anyone would have inevitably been bitten except those who knew how to handle snakes.

But its opponent was Red-faced Mongoose.

Before it could get in contact with him, Gebu had grabbed it by its neck by reaching out his hand out as swift as whirlwind.

The wrathful king cobra stiffened up its body, raised its front quarters, and whipped its tail from side to side.

The black tail flew about in the air like a whip with an attempt to lasso Gebu's neck.

It wanted to strangle Gebu to death.

Quick as a wink, Gebu flung the king cobra clamped in his hand up to the ceiling, which it hit hard before it bounced back and crashed to the floor.

Suddenly, with a whoosh, the king cobra raised its front part. Facing Gebu, it was ready to fight him again.

Gebu lunged forward and attacked it with both his hands and feet. With the former, he got hold of the cobra's neck; with the latter, he stepped on its tail. He began to play his trump card once again: pulling the cobra up with his hands while pressing it down with his feet.

The king cobra became motionless.

Gebu then shook it by the throat until it was loosened like an elastic rope.

Suddenly, Gebu knitted his brows tightly together.

Why did the king cobra fly in through the window?

Without wings, the cobra can't fly.

Someone must have thrown it in!

Who did it then?

Why did he do so?

Did he try to kill me with its venom?

He barely gave out a scream of an alarm when he looked at the cobra closely…

There were no venomous fangs in its wide-open mouth!

He examined it further and found the fangs already removed.

The unique scars left on the fang sheaths told him that he himself had removed the fangs.

A thought immediately dawned upon Gebu:

Isn't this cobra the one I gave the boy?

Didn't I remove the fangs myself?

Yes, it is exactly the same cobra.

So, it must be the boy that threw it through the window, mustn't it?

It's him.

It must be him!

Gebu leaned well out of the window.

It was pitch dark outside.

The whole horse caravan inn was immersed in silence.

He threw the cobra in while I was about to drink the wine. What was he trying to tell me?

Hm…a snake?

A venomous one!

A snake that is poisonous.

Can it be that the wine is laced with poison?

The thought petrified Gebu…

Is this probable?

The wine was a gift from Boss Lu.

It was delivered by the inn assistant Langzhe.

Is it possible…?

Gebu looked around…

Everything that was unlike to happen had happened:

The salt merchant Ni Sebo was lying face down, dead.

Chapter 13

Ni Sebo was not dead. He merely lost consciousness.

Lying on the bed, he appeared natural and stable, without the slightest sign of painful struggle due to death by poisoning.

After further observation, Gebu came to a new conclusion...

Instead of poison, the wine was laced with a sleeping potion that put people out temporarily.

"Don't think you're in a safe when you stay in the Loquat Horse Caravan Inn!"

The Scarface's dismal voice rang in Gebu's ears again.

Only at this very moment did he realize that Scarface's warning was out of the ordinary.

The inn is indeed not safe.

Boss Lu provided the wine.

Langzhe served the wine.

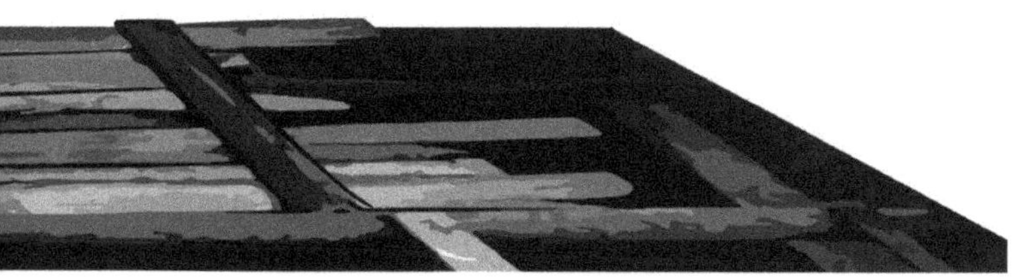

Who laced the wine with the sleeping potion then?

It could be one or both of them. Or even a third person unrelated to them.

The way Langzhe declined to drink the wine seemed to show that he was aware of the potion in it. But he looked very innocent at the same time.

He even drank a whole cup!

In front of his mind's eye flashed again Boss Lu's triangle face with a pair of medium-sized, round eyes.

Boss Lu had been running the inn for many years, treating his guests with honesty and sincerity. He also talked civilly and amiably. Could he lace the wine with the sleeping potion?

Gebu knitted his eyebrows tightly.

He made up his mind almost in a blink of an eye.

Gebu then threw the king cobra out of the window. He set it free because it was his savior.

Then, he picked up the cup filled with the wine, shut his mouth tight, and poured the wind out of the cup, allowing the liquid to stream from his mouth down to his chest.

He left a little wind in the cup.

The bamboo tube cup was pretty deep, and if he had emptied it, he would have given himself away.

When he got everything ready, he bent his head back and lay down on the bed diagonally, pretending to be in a sleeping stupor.

His mouth smelling wine, his body tainted with wine, and lying askew and motionless in bed, with Ni Sebo's lying genuinely unconscious by his side, Gebu looked indeed knocked out by the potion-laced wine.

By beating it in their own game, Gebu wanted to figure out the next move to be made by anyone who had laced the wine.

With his eyes closed, he visualized the boy again, seeing him snorting a resentment at him before he disappeared.

What a smart boy!

He protected me in secret, came to my rescue when I was in danger, but he never answered my questions directly, making everything a mystery.

"Uncle, the person you're looking for has been murdered."

His words are completely from the mouth of an insider.

Who's the insider behind this boy?

Why didn't he meet me face to face?

Is there something wrong with me that has caused his vigilance?

While he was thinking, he heard the rustling footsteps outside the door.

Someone tiptoed over.

The footfalls stopped outside the door.

He must be peeping into the room through the crack of the door.

"They're both knocked out!"

Gebu heard a murmuring conversation.

Obviously, two people came.

After waiting for a while, the bamboo door was finally pushed open with a squeak.

The kerosene hurricane lamp hanging on the bamboo pole was very bright.

Gebu did not venture to open his eyes.

The two men came directly to him…

I'm their target, and I was the one the potion was meant for.

Soon, a cold hand was pressed against Gebu's forehead and then pushed his head aside slightly.

Gebu shook his head with the momentum and gave the impression that his neck was as soft as cotton.

The one who pushed him said,

"It's okay now. Let's carry him to the cave first and wait and see what we're going to do with him when Green Bamboo Viper comes."

Green Bamboo Viper!

Green Bamboo Viper again!

Gebu's heart skipped a beat.

He heard this terrifying name again.

"Carry him to the cave?"

What cave?

Can it be Green Bamboo Viper's headquarters?

The two men carried Gebu by his arms and legs up from the bed and out of the one-room house.

The night breeze was chilly.

Gebu stole a glance at the two men in front of and at the back of him.

Both had their faces masked with black cloth.

The medium-sized man carrying him by his legs looked very familiar.

He stole another look trying to identify him.

He was facing away from Gebu. The gait and the slightly plump stature…

Gee! Gebu recognized him as the plump inn assistant Langzhe!

The guy drank the wine under my nose and was soon able to carry me.

It seems his antidote to be really effective!

Now it's clear that Langzhe is an accomplice of Green Bamboo Viper.

Then, what about Boss Lu.

The two thugs, one in his front and the other behind him, carried him through a loquat grove and to a small house. They unlocked it and entered.

Gebu was shocked!

What? The cave is in the small house?

And it's on the premise of the horse caravan inn?

Sure enough! After carrying Gebu into the room, the two thugs put him down, and pulled open a big trunk on the floor to reveal the opening of a dark cave.

Gebu was carried into it.

It was lit by a kerosene hurricane lamp.

In the dim lamplight, Gebu secretly surveyed the cave.

To his surprise, he found the cave having a small opening but a big cavity. There were quite a few things piled and heaped in it, in addition to a bed covered with bed sheets, a table, and a few stools.

The cave was permeated with the stench of tobacco, indicating that someone had just smoked here.

It's impossible for Boss Lu not to know such a mysterious cave in his horse caravan inn.

Perhaps, he's the owner of the cave.

Perhaps, he's Green Bamboo Viper!

As he was being carried to the depth of the cave, he gave a shudder.

He saw something he wanted to see!

And he was extremely shocked when he saw them.

Against the earthen wall of the cave was lying a row of four horseback loads.

Gee, four horseback loads!

He found part of the straw matting wrapping one of the loads already messed up a bit.

He thought it likely for someone to have taken something out without covering it properly afterwards.

Gebu was being carried by, nearly brushing the loads.

He took a glance at the contents inside the improperly covered opening of the load.

The glance caused his heart to jump into his throat:

Firearms!

Gebu saw firearms!

They were all machineguns!

A full horseback load of machineguns!

Without a doubt, these are the four horseback loads reported missing by Weng Guo in his secret letter.

Weng Guo's judgment was verified: the loads were indeed filled with firearms.

Trafficked in by Iron's Head across the border, they were ready to be delivered to Mountain Wind.

Everything was clear now.

The two drug lords were in secret contact with the help of Green Bamboo Viper hiding in Caoluo Street.

The Loquat Horse Caravan Inn was their liaison station, as well as their station for transferring weapons and drugs.

Now, the four loads of firearms have arrived at the transfer station.

Next, either Mountain Wind would dispatch someone to pick them up or Green Bamboo Viper had to find ways to deliver them to him in the mountain.

To prevent the firearms from being intercepted like last time, they had gone out of their way to make the arrangements as carefully as possible.

With his eyes better adjusted to the near darkness, he discovered something that surprised him again:

All the four horseback loads were tied with red cloth ribbons.

Gosh! Big red cloth ribbons!

Swarthy Guotou's chuckles instantly rang in his ears:

"Ha-ha-ha! Those red cloth ribbons are the marks I've made to the loads. I don't want other caravan's loads to be confused with these because they're army provisions."

Why do these four loads of weapons also have the same big red cloth ribbons as Swarthy Guotou's?

Not only is the marking identical, but they are also tied in the middle into the "hero's knot" like a turban-like headwear.

What's going on?

Is Swarthy Guotou also one of Green Bamboo Viper's men?

There're only two possibilities…

The first is that Swarthy Guotou does belong to Green Bamboo Viper's gang. Early tomorrow morning, he'll set out with his train of horses to deliver the army provisions to the prefectural capital via the path at the foot of Mount Nanla. He may take the opportunity to unload the four loads of firearms mixed with the other loads so that Mountain Wind's men can pick them up.

The other possibility is that Swarthy Guotou is an honest horse-puller, ignorant of the illegal dealings going on in the Loquat Horse Caravan Inn. It's Green Bamboo Viper that has secretly replaced four of Swarthy Guotou's loads of army provisions with his loads of firearms disguised to resemble Swarthy Guotou's. Then the loads of firearms would be shipped out of Caoluo Street with no one knowing it. It'll be a cinch for the weapons to get into the hands of Mountain Wind. Either Mountain Wind is informed beforehand so that he'll ambush the caravan under the pretext of looting the provisions and take the firearms with him or, as Swarthy Guotou told him, the two militiamen, who are Green Bamboo Viper's men, will find ways to keep the four loads of arm with them at the foot of Mount Nanla.

From all the clues and traces he had gathered, Gebu leaned toward the second possibility.

Whichever possibility means the same: the four loads of firearms will be mixed with the army provisions and shipped out of Caoluo Street tomorrow morning.

This is a top-secret operation!

The success of the operation is vital both to the shipment of the firearms into the mountain and to the survival of the secret liaison station in the Loquat Horse Caravan Inn.

Green Bamboo Viper must have racked his brains making all the arrangements.

By assassinating Weng Guo, he's ridded themselves of the first big obstacle to his operation.

It can be inferred that he had no choice but to do so.

That is to say, he already knew that Weng Guo had wind of their secret operation and especially of the four horseback loads. Therefore, he had to take this risky step.

Then, what about his treatment of me? Gebu asked himself.

This extremely sensitive Green Bamboo Viper must have smelled a little something suspicious about me.

Perhaps, he began to suspect and keep an eye on me when he found out that I was looking for Weng Guo as soon as I arrived at Caoluo Street.

That night, he learned from his accomplices that I was not sleeping in the horse caravan inn.

At the same time, the killing of the corpse-carrying "hairy devils" at the dry riverbed deepened Green Bamboo Viper's suspicion of me.

He may suspect that I killed the "hairy devil," but he's still not certain.

That's because my makeup worked perfectly.

Then, to figure out my true identification, he tried to capture me alive with all the means he could think of.

Eventually, he did it: I was "dosed" out.

But why didn't Green Bamboo Viper kill me like he had murdered Weng Guo?

There may be two inferred answers to the question:

The first answer to the question why Green Bamboo Viper is not eager to kill me is that he wants to know the real purpose of my coming to Caoluo Street. He wants to find out if I'm aware of the Loquat Horse Caravan Inn's secret. If I am, am I here to investigate what I was informed of before coming to Caoluo Street or I just stumbled upon the secret after I checked into the inn. If it's the first case, then the Loquat Horse Caravan Inn is exposed, and he must make a prompt decision.

The second answer is that Green Bamboo Viper really thinks of me as an itinerary snake merchant. He's doubts result from his oversensitivity. He's doing everything he can to learn about me so that he can allay his suspicion.

But both the answers involved a puzzle that Gebu could not solve no matter how hard he tried. What puzzled him was that Green Bamboo Viper seemed to have shown a special interest in his life, the life of an "innocent man."

It's safely to say that Green Bamboo Viper never has a qualm about killing an innocent person at random.

He can do so as long as he sees fit.

But this time, he's been behaving differently. It seems that there's something secret that he can't tell, something that's hindering him from taking reckless actions.

Then, what is that secret something…?

Gebu was pondering, trying to get his thoughts to shape, when he heard Langzhe whisper,

"Well, why can't we stab the guy to death? Why do we have to go through so many troubles?"

The other thug grumbled,

"You're right. I've no idea why our otherwise decisive boss is so hesitant this time."

See, these two thugs and I think alike.

As they chattered, the thugs stopped to place Gebu on the floor.

Gebu could not help wondering…

Who in the world is Green Bamboo Viper?

As the secret liaison station is located in his Loquat Horse Caravan Inn, there's a great chance that Green Bamboo Viper is Boss Lu.

However, after analyzing all the happenings, Gebu found it likely that Green Bamboo Viper was the aspiration-like Scarface.

I must find out who Green Bamboo Viper is and send the information to the anti-drug police as soon as possible so that they can destroy this secret liaison station for the drug lords from both sides of the border and remove the obstacle to the extermination of Mountain Wind and his gang.

The thought heightened his fighting spirit as well as his anxiety.

Early tomorrow morning, the firearms will be shipped out mixed with the army provisions. The situation is urgent, but I can't get myself free at the moment.

Obviously, trying to intercept the firearms myself is a mission impossible.

But the possible helping hand Kaluo is not available at this moment of dire need.

Gebu kind of regretted not telling Kaluo the purpose of his coming to Caoluo Street and asking him for help when he met with him in the mountain.

What can I do at this critical moment?

Gebu was feeling anxious when suddenly he heard something astir at the opening of the cave.

Someone was descending into the cave.

Gebu heard his footfalls.

The footfalls sounded so familiar that he seemed to have heard them somewhere else.

Gebu's heart skipped a beat.

Who is he?

Gebu opened his eyes slightly in secret.

But the slightly plump body of Langzhe blocked his view.

Gebu could not move because he was still "unconscious."

He expected the man who had just come down to walk further into his field of vision.

Unfortunately, he stopped, never to move further.

…as if he had chosen the angle where Langzhe could shield him.

Gebu sighed silently.

He then pricked his ears up—

Ears as sensitive as those of a red-faced mongoose.

When he could not use his eyes, his ears would compensate for their lost function.

Finally, he heard the newcomer speak.

"This is not a good location. Take him to the old place."

How familiar the voice was!

Gebu's heart skipped another beat.

The voice was deep and thick, and hardly audible, but it sounded as if it were the rumble of muffled thunder rolling over his heart.

After he finished, the man went out of the cave.

Gebu was picked up by the two thugs.

When he was carried to the opening of the cave, he peered at the muddy ground secretly.

His effort was by no means in vain.

He saw the footprints in the mud clearly.

The two thugs carried Gebu out of the cave and placed him on a horse-drawn cart. They then covered him with some banana leaves.

The horse-drawn cart began to roll.

Soon, Gebu realized what the "old place" meant.

The deafening splashing of water, the uneven pebble road, and the dry bed of Nanla River.

So, this was the old place.

It seemed that someone had been waiting.

As soon as he was placed on the riverbed, Gebu heard someone issuing an order,

"Untie him quickly!"

Before opening his eyes, Gebu had already known from the voice who had given the order. He was none other than the little old man who had claimed that he had snakes to sell him.

Chapter 14

The tipsy look demonstrated at the tangyuan eatery was nowhere to be found in the little old man's mung-been like eyes.

After some bitter antidote was forced into his mouth, Gebu pretended to gain consciousness. Then he was pressed to his knees on the ground by the two thugs who had carried him. Now they pressed him down by lifting his arms high behind him.

In the dim moonlight, he saw the little old man's mung-bean eyes chilling and ferocious.

The ferocious look resembled that of a green bamboo viper during its attack.

Gebu snorted, "Where, where am I?"

The little old man answered unhurriedly with a drawl:

"By the river! We've got cool breeze here that awakened you up from the wine."

Gebu blinked his eyes and breathed heavily, exhaling his pent-up anger. He turned to look at the two people holding up his arms and found the one on the left to be Langzhe.

The one on the right was Horse Face, who had posed as a militiaman.

"What…what are you doing?"

Gebu feigned ignorance.

The little old man came forward and said, "Gebu, we've startled you again!"

Staring at him, Gebu said, "Is it you? I've been looking for you. You told me you had snakes to sell and asked me to wait under the banyan tree…"

The little old man cut him short:

"Stop beating about the bush and forget about the snake business! You think I'm a fool, eh? Tell me the truth!"

"What? What truth?" Gebu asked blinking his eyes, "What I said was the truth. What're you up to?"

The little old man rolled his mung-bean eyes and interrogated, "What am I up to? Let me ask you what on earth are you doing?"

"I'm a snake merchant! Didn't you want to sell your snakes to me?"

"Stop your nonsense! Let me ask you. Is seeing Weng Guo part of your snake business?"

"What fruit?[11]" Gebu widened his eyes and asked, "Is it sour or sweet?"

Suppressing his anger, the little old man said, "Don't play dumb with me! I'll twist your head off and place it in the vase like the woman of the magician's troupe!"

"Humph, don't try to scare me. I'm not afraid of you!" shouted Gebu. Then he grinned, "I really don't know what Weng fruit is."

"Weng Guo isn't a fruit. He's a man, living in the little house under the banyan tree. You went to see him as soon as you came to town. Tell me why!"

"Oh, you mean the household under the banyan tree. I've been there. I've been there. I was there not to see Weng Guo, but to see Zhuang Laohan's brother Zhuang Laoyao. I went to the wrong address. I haven't found Zhuang Laoyao yet."

Gebu intentionally confused the two Zhuang brothers' names and repeated Zhuang Laoyao for emphasis.

He discovered that the little old man showed no reaction to this egregious mistake. On the contrary, he was quite attentive while listening to him, without the slightest display of boredom.

What? The little old man isn't aware of my pretended effort to look for Zhuang Laohan, is he?

Sure enough, the little old man began:

"Where did you come up with a Zhuang Laoyao? Stop hemming and hawing with me. I'm not confused at all."

---

[11] "Guo," the first name of Weng Guo, means "fruit."

Is the little old man really unaware of this?

Why so?

Didn't Scarface tell him about it?

Could it be…

Gebu immediately found something unusual in this Zhuang Laohan story. Therefore, he changed the subject at once: "What I said is the truth, nothing but the truth. I really don't know Weng Guo. I'm here in Caoluo Street to do my snake business."

The little old man smirked,

"Since you didn't know him, why did you kill him?"

"Aah!" Gebu looked horrified, "Don't you accuse the wrong person!"

"You really look as innocent as you pretend to be! Tell me this. If you didn't kill Weng Guo, why did you go and see him the night you arrived in Caoluo Street?"

"What? The more you ask, the more confused I am. I went to Weng Guo's house? Don't try to scare me. I'm just a snake merchant, and I know nothing."

"Stop yelling!" The little old man began to lose patience, "Even if you don't know anything, you should know this, shouldn't you?"

With that, he pulled open his shirt and from a small leather box on his leather belt, he produced a little glass bottle.

The two thugs pressed Gebu down and squeezed him between their legs so that he was unable to move.

The little old man flashed the glass bottle in front of Gebu's eyes.

"You're a snake handler, and you must know what venom this is. How about prying your eyes open and dropping a little bit into them? So, do you want to keep your eyes or tell the truth?"

Saying so, the little old man lunged a step forward and reached out his eagle-claw like hand to lift Gebu's eyelids.

A grave test of courage and sacrifice suddenly presented itself to Gebu.

A drop of the venom will destroy my eyesight.

But I'd rather die than tell what the little old man wants to know.

Gebu firmly believed that what Green Bamboo Viper wanted direly was not his life but his confession.

So long as I can survive this ordeal, so long as I still breathe, I'll crawl back to the anti-drug police station to inform them of the thugs even without my eyes.

To live and to accomplish the mission, I must stick to what I have told them no matter what ordeals I have to go through.

"Tell me what on earth are you here for? Why did you come to Caoluo Street?"

The little old man held the glass bottle up and aimed it at Gebu's eyes.

He had turned into a demon.

Gebu ceased to pretend being panic-stricken. Instead,

he erected his back.

"I'm a snake merchant and came to Caoluo Street to scape a living. In the line of my business, I've been dead many times. Bring it on!"

Before he finished, he saw the flash of the bottle!

Instantly…

He felt his eyes pricked by a thousand needles and his heart pierced by a thousand arrows!

"Ouch!"

With a sharp scream, he started shivering all over involuntarily.

The two masked thugs pinched him tightly between them.

Gebu writhed his neck back and forth in agony.

Beads of sweat dripped from his face distorted with pain.

The little old man waved the bottle in front of him.

"If you tell me the truth, I'll spare the other eye. Be honest! You still have time!"

Bearing the pain and panting, Gebu said, "I beg you to spare the other eye so that I can live by doing my snake business."

The little old man suddenly blurted out: "Drag him to the water."

The two thugs dragged Gebu to the edge of the river and pressed his head into the water.

The chilly water rushed over his head and washed his

face, as well as his eyes.

The pain seemed to ease up. Gebu opened his eyes in the water.

To his astonishment, he could still see the dim moonlight shone upon the water surface.

What? I'm not blind?

What was going on?

"No, you're not blind." The little old man edged up beaming, "What's in the bottle is not venom. It's chili solution. You didn't expect it, did you? Eyes are the most precious things a man have. How can I meddle with them? Besides, I have prepared an interesting magic show for you. It's worth watching than the 'Beauty in the Vase'!"

As soon as he finished, the thugs carried Gebu up, dragged him away from the edge of the water, and pressed him down to kneel on the dry riverbed of pebbles.

The little old man clapped three times.

With the clapping, two figures walked out from behind a rock as big as a lying buffalo.

Or rather, it was a burly man pushing another person out from behind the Lying-buffalo Rock.

That person had his hands tied behind him.

When he came close to Gebu...

Good Heavens!

Gebu hardly screamed.

It was none other than the nameless boy!

Gebu saw his face covered with blood stains, his mouth stuffed with a towel, one of his eyes swollen, and his clothes torn into tatters. They must have injured one of his legs as he limped when he walked.

The poor child had been beaten to a pulp.

However, he was still holding his head high with obstinacy and pride, and from his eyes shot out the light of defiance.

He staggered over on the uneven pebbles, the dim moonlight that shone on his thin and lanky body casting an even skinnier shadow on the riverbed.

Gebu felt so painful that his heart ached and his eyes were blurred with tears...

He had never expected that he should meeti the boy again in such a fashion.

He's suffered so much all because of me!

Gebu bit his lip tight.

Salt-tasting blood seeped from his lip and filled his mouth.

He felt sorry for the ordeal his appearance and action have put the boy through.

No matter how many tears would not undo the tortures.

He wanted to throw himself upon him and hold him tight in his arms.

But it was impossible.

Watching the boy drawing near, Gebu wanted to send him a message of gratitude, guilt, and solace through his look.

When the boy came close enough, Gebu found that he was gazing at the starry sky instead of looking at him.

Yes, at the sky filled with stars!

Gebu felt his heart missing a beat.

Suddenly, the words of the company commander of the anti-drug police began to ring in his ears once more:

"Never feel for anyone, even including me, because feelings can soften your heart."

At first, Gebu thought of the company commander's words as sensible.

Indeed, feelings can make people softhearted.

However, at such a moment, how could Gebu's heart be hardened in the face of a tortured and unyielding boy?

Gebu was agonizing at the thought; he was so agonizing that hands trembled uncontrollably.

The little old man planted himself between Gebu and the boy, his mung-bean little eyes ping-ponging from the boy to Gebu.

"Well, I can see that you guys know each other. He ran away from behind your hotel room like a startled fawn. Gebu, what did you tell him? Or what did he tell you, eh?"

Gebu leered at the little old man.

"Of course," the little old man nodded, "you hate me, and you won't confess. As for him? He also refused to confess. He's a rascal! Young as he is, he clams up with his mouth as firm as the bill of a duck! But, you must be a man and spill it. A man of your stature should claim responsibility for what you've done. How can you be so unmanly as to involve such a tender young child?"

Glaring at the little old man, Gebu tried hard to suppress his wrath.

"I know you're fond of and sympathetic with the boy," said the little old man still unhurriedly. "But I've got to do what I've got to. It's all because you both refuse to confess. You see, when he was beaten, he didn't cry because his mouth was stuffed. Maybe you want to hear him cry, don't you? Probably, the screams for pain and calls for mercy when a child was severely beaten can soften your heart of iron and stone and make you tell the truth, right? So, only you can save this poor child from his misery!"

The little old man paused, glancing at Gebu first, and then at the boy.

Silence reigned.

On the river splashed.

"Okay, none of you want to speak. As saying goes that a stone will shed tears when it hears a child cry. Now, let's put the saying to a test. Hey, you guys, gouge the boy's eyes out!"

With the little old man's howling, the burly man behind the boy stepped up and grabbed the boy by his collar. He then kicked him so hard at the back of his knees that the boy dropped on them involuntarily on the pebble riverbed with a thud. The man then bent the boy's head back by pulling his hair.

The man held up his other hand, ready to plunge it into the boy's eye sockets like the claws of an eagle…

A tragedy was about to strike on the dry riverbed covered

in the dim moonlight.

Gebu saw clearly…

The five fingers of the big hand reaching toward the boy's eyes were as sharp as awls.

Gebu saw clearly…

The eyes meeting the awls were as bright as the stars.

The burly man's five fingers were quivering!

But the boy's eyes were by no means blinking!

The river held its flow.

The moon dulled its light.

A bloody tragedy was imminent.

The boy's scream would soon tear the darkness of the night open.

Gebu roared:

"Hold your hand!"

His roar sounded like thunder crashing above the head. Startled, the burly man withdrew his hand. Shocked, the little old man pronked like an antelope.

"Okay, okay, hold it! Hold it!" As he waved to the burly man, the little old man turned to Gebu with his smirking face,

"So, you've got something to say?"

Gebu heaved a pent-up sigh of anger, his eyes glaring as if they were on fire.

"I'm responsible for what I've done. It has nothing to do with this boy. Let him go!"

The little old man's eyes twinkled cunningly:

"Good, you're a man! Responsible for what you've done yourself!"

He then turned to the burly man and ordered,

"Set the boy free!"

The man released his grip.

The boy rose to his feet.

Just then, Gebu saw the boy turning his head toward, his big eyes fixed on him.

The boy's eyes were filled with alarm.

No, also with questioning and resentment!

Gebu's heart was almost broken.

The little old man went up to Gebu and asked:

"I just want to know who you are and what you are here at Caoluo Street for."

"I…"

Gebu could not say it.

How could he?

And what did he say?

Gebu's face was reddened with predicament.

He wished to swallow the little old man up.

"You still refuse to confess and want to fool me with your snake business nonsense, right? Fine! I'll let you hear the scream from the boy!"

The burly man reached to grab the boy.

At this juncture, something unexpected happened:

Like a leopard cub breaking out of a cage, the boy turned and dashed toward the Lying-buffalo Rock behind him.

The burly man failed to get hold him...

Bam!

The boy bumped his head into the rock like a tree falling, a house collapsing, a mountain crumbling, and the earth cracking!

"My...child..."

Gebu shrieked like mad, tears swelling from his eyes.

His sorrowful shriek slit the night sky.

The teary echo reached to the mountains far and wide.

The faraway mountains shook.

The faraway mountains wept.

The sorrowful shriek was bounced and rebounded among the rolling, deep, and faraway mountains:

"My...good boy..."

"My...good boy..."

The boy could not hear Gebu crying.

Nor could he hear the call of the faraway mountains.

Lying on the cold riverbed, he looked as if he were sleeping...

Chapter 15

Seeing the boy bump into the Lying-buffalo Rock, the little old man heaved a sigh.

Producing a lighter from his pocket, he clicked the igniter.

The dazzling flame jumped up high and bright.

Before he lit his cigarette…

Bang!

A report of a gunshot came from the riverbed.

It was closely followed by a hubbub of voices and a commotion of footfalls.

A group of armed men came running.

Peering at where the hues and cries came, the little old man left Gebu a word:

"Argh, you killed Weng Guo and try to deny it. We can't let you off!"

Then, tossing his head to the thugs, he screamed,

"Run!"

Leaving Gebu behind, the thugs scattered in all directions.

Seeing the thugs dispersing, the people came running also spread out in their pursuit. As they chased, they yelled.

Gebu rushed to the Lying-buffalo Rock and picked up the boy.

"My good boy! My good boy…"

The boy's heart had ceased beating.

His body was as soft as cotton.

Blood was dripping from his smashed forehead.

With his quivering hand, Gebu lifted the front of his shirt and wiped the blood gently off his forehead.

Tears swelled in his eyes again.

He pressed his cheek tight on the boy's dainty face, which was now as cold as a stone.

"…my good boy, my good boy. I…I don't even know your name…!"

Gebu's shoulders twitched with painful sorrow.

Just then, he heard footfalls approaching closer and closer.

The footfalls came from a pair of brand-new rubber-sole shoes crunching on the pebbles, sounding sturdy and elastic.

Gebu raised his head and saw a man walking up to him in the dim moonlight.

The moonlight revealed a square face, on which there was a nose of a prominent bridge and a pair of thin almond eyes matched with a pair of caterpillar-like brows above them.

It was no one else but Kaluo!

"Gebu!"

Kaluo called him and hurried over.

Gebu carefully laid the boy on the ground and rose to greet Kaluo.

"Hey, Bother Kaluo! Is that you?"

Kaluo rushed over and put his arms around Gebu.

"Are you okay, Gebu?"

Gebu shook his head.

"Luckily, I got my guts from snake hunting. Otherwise, I wouldn't be able to see you!"

"Sorry for putting you in harm's way alone!"

"Back from home?"

"Yes! I rushed back after I fixed my sick wife and children up. I arrived at Caoluo Street in the evening. Before I had time to see you in the inn, I had learned about Weng Guo's assassination and went to his residence. On my way, a man who had been hand fishing ran up to me and told me that some people were committing a violent crime on the riverbed. So, I immediately rushed over with the others. We caught the little old man, and the rest will be caught eventually!"

Hi face brightened, Gebu asked, "You caught the little old man?"

Kaluo nodded, "He said he was interrogating you."

"Did he tell you what he did that for?"

"He forced you to admit that you killed Weng Guo, didn't he?"

"I think that was what he meant to an extent, but I don't know who Weng Guo is."

"The little old man confessed. He killed Weng Guo."

His eyes wide open, Gebu said, "What? What does he do? Why did he have to kill Weng Guo?"

Kaluo said, "They're drug dealers. They hated Weng Guo because he had intercepted their drugs. They murdered him while I was away. To cover themselves up, they tried to shift the blame on you, because you're an itinerary merchant. They picked you as their scapegoat."

Squinting his eyes, Gebu said, "I see. No wonder I started to fight for my life as soon as I arrived for reasons I didn't even know ..."

Kaluo said nodding, "It was because of all the traps they set."

He had barely finished when a chilling voice boomed in the dark,

"No! It's you who set the traps!"

Gee! The startling voice was so dismal that it sounded

as if creeping from the ground.

Both Kaluo and Gebu were astounded at once.

Before Kaluo turned around, Gebu had already spotted a terrifying face emerging from behind him.

The face was as cold as an iron ingot.

A lump of iron ore!

The pale moonlight showed a knife scar on the face, a scar that ran from the top of the forehead down to where the eyebrows met.

Scarface!

Kaluo turned around and saw Scarface as well. Meanwhile, he also caught sight of two dark muzzles pointed at him.

Scarface held two handguns.

Silence prevailed…

For a second, the three men froze like statues.

Silence persisted.

Only the current of the Nanla River splashed breathtakingly.

Scarface stood still, fixing his eyes on Kaluo and Gebu.

"Lao Meng! Lao Meng! What are you doing?"

Scarface, who was nicknamed Lao Meng, which means "Old Mongoose," pointed both his guns at Kaluo and asked, "You still don't know what I'm doing?"

Scarface had barely finished when all of a sudden Kaluo dodged to the side, away from the muzzles of the guns. He yelled, "Help me, Gebu!"

At the same, he pulled his gun out from the front of his shirt.

He was about to aim it at Scarface when a kick flew over and knocked it off his hand.

Kaluo was stunned…

The kick was launched by Gebu!

"Catch it!" Scarface shouted to Gebu.

Following the shout, something whished toward him.

Scarface threw one of his handguns to Gebu.

Slam!

Gebu caught it in the air.

The gun, once in his hands, took him by surprise:

It was exactly the one that he had buried in the grass at the base of the broad-leaved tree.

It dawned upon him instantly…

When he was burying the gun, Lao Meng was concealing himself in the forest, where he also saw him concealing the kemu tally in his headwear. Spying in hiding, he also saw him chatting cordially with Kaluo on the mountain path.

All of this aroused Lao Meng's suspicion.

He could not figure out their relationship.

Therefore, he also included Gebu in his list under his surveillance.

Now everything is clear!

Gebu was pointing his gun at Kaluo.

With two dark muzzles almost dug into his chest and

back, Kaluo trembled all over.

He turned around and said to Scarface, "Lao Meng, Lao Meng, please, please stop pulling my legs..."

Lao Meng said, "Who's pulling your legs? When you discovered that Weng Guo knew something about the Loquat Horse Caravan Inn's secret, you planned the assassination. To cover your hide, you pretended to go home to visit your allegedly sick wife and children before your operation. In fact, you never left. You turned back as soon as you reached the mountain pass and hid in the horse caravan inn all the time. There, you saw to it that Weng Guo was terminated. You thought your secret would be kept by getting rid of Weng Guo, but you never expected he had sent a secret letter to the anti-drug polite. He had also told me his suspicion of you at the same time. Now, I can tell you, your subordinate Boss Lu, as well as the salt merchant Ni Sebo dispatched by Mountain Wind to pick up the firearms—they have all been under our surveillance. Although we haven't seen the four loads of firearms yet, I'm convinced they must be in the horse caravan inn.

On hearing Lao Meng's remark, Kaluo looked at Gebu with an entreating look.

"Brother Gebu, Brother Gebu, don't listen to his nonsense. He's crazy!"

Kaluo's look was so familiar.

Suddenly, what had happened six years before flashed back across his mind's eye: after offending drug dealers, he fled to Gebu. He had the same entreating look in his eyes when Gebu opened the door to receive him.

But today…

Pointing his gun at Kaluo, Gebu squeezed out three words between his teeth:

"Green—Bamboo—Viper!"

Hearing the three words, Kaluo was struck dumb.

If I'm not wrong, you started drug trafficking as early as six years ago. Due to an infight, you made enemies of another drug gang. After you fled to my house to avoid being hunted down by them, you secretly threw in your lot with Mountain Wind, becoming his liaison with Iron's Head. Just now, I heard your footsteps and your voice in the cave where the four horseback loads of firearms were hidden, and I saw the footprints of your new rubber-sole shoes. Because you are my parallel cousin, I certainly wished everything were an illusion, but…"

Giving him a grim look, Kaluo said to Gebu with a snort, "Don't mention the word 'cousin.' What cousinhood or brotherhood do you know, eh? If you were not my cousin, you couldn't expect to live till this day. You'd better appreciate how I treat you as my kinsman."

Gebu gave a shudder. So, this was Green Bamboo Viper's unspoken secret that has prevented him from taking his life!

Gebu said, "I've already appreciated your relative's goodwill. It's true you didn't kill me because I'm your cousin, for which I'm grateful. But if I had told you my identity and my mission on my way to Caoluo Street or if I had failed to endure the little old man's torment and disclosed to him who I am and what I do, then what would have come to pass? I'm afraid you would not have allowed me to live for a single minute. But I insisted that I were a snake merchant, and the little old man had to signal you by igniting his lighter so that you could come to see me for yourself and try to keep me in the dark again. So, this is what you mean by your cousinly or brotherly affection?"

"Forget it," Kaluo said with a wave of his hand, "I know who you're and what you're doing here now. I went over to Mountain Wind to survive. Now that I'm your captive, this is my destined fate, for which I've no regret. But you, working with the anti-drug police, you'll regret it sooner or later…"

Gebu sneered:

"So, this is how you see my job?"

Kaluo responded, "Yes. You often said, 'A rabbit's tail is short, but life is long,' didn't you? You'll suffer some day. For the sake of our cousinship, please give me a way out: let me drown in the river myself."

Gebu swiped his hand around him and said, "Even I gave you the consent, I'm afraid they won't."

Only then did Kaluo see militiamen all around. They had positioned themselves in an encirclement without his notice.

Each aimed a rifle at him silently.

"Fine! Gebu, let me repeat what I told you six years ago, 'There are rocks where there are mountains; there's rain where there're rivers. So long as I'm still alive, we're bound to see each other again!'"

As he finished, Kaluo closed his eyes.

Lao Meng went up to Gebu and produced something from the front of his shirt.

"This is what Weng Guo hid in a salt jar. He only told me about it."

Taking it over in his hand, Gebu found it to be the other half of the kemu tally with an arrowhead carved on it.

He placed the two halves together, and an arrow appeared...

An arrow in its entirety!

Suddenly, Swarthy Guotou's words rung in his ears again:

"Just go to him. His bark is worse than his bite, so to speak. You won't be disappointed. In my opinion, he must have scared all the girls away with his barks and remains a single, as single as a tree."

Oh, Weng Guo, my good bro! Now I understand why you used such an ancient and odd method of communication. I'm here with the other half, but you can't hear me calling you...

Gnashing his teeth, Gebu clenched the kemu tightly in his hand.

When he looked up, he caught sight of Lao Meng crouching in front of the boy lying on his back by the Lying-buffalo Rock. He was rubbing the boy's face gently and silently.

His hand was so gentle, as if the boy were asleep, and he

was afraid to wake him up.

Gebu's heart suddenly weighed as heavy as a crag.

He walked quietly to Lao Meng and crouched down, fixing his eyes on the boy's broad forehead, jutting chin, tenuous nasal bridge, and slightly thick lips.

His eyes closed tight.

But Gebu seemed to see the big, dark eyes twinkling like stars again.

He seemed to hear their conversation when they first met:

"…, Child, what's your name?"

"If I tell you my name, do you think you'll believe me?"

"I trust that you won't fool me."

"Maybe I will. You'd better not ask."

"What? Why?"

"We're not friends!"

Everything has become bygones.

And bygone days can never return.

Heaving a deep sigh, Gebu said to Lao Meng:

"Lao Meng, the boy died for the sake of me, but I don't even know his name."

Instead of responding, Lao Meng kept caressing the boy's face.

Gebu asked again, "Lao Meng, do you know him?"

Lao Meng nodded.

"What's his name?"

"Xiao Meng."

Young Mongoose!?

Lao Meng, Xiao Meng…Old Mongoose, Young Mongoose…

Are they…?

Gebu asked hastily:

"He's your son?"

Lao Meng remained reticent.

But, in the dim moonlight, Gebu saw his eyes glistening.

They were tears swelling in his eyes!

They were tears that were not dripping.

First written in Luxi, Yunnan Province, September 1984

Revised in the western suburbs of Beijing, April 2018